HATRED, ANGER
DESPAIR . . . HATRED . . .

1:30 a.m., Saturday: Sixty-two inmates in Dormitory E-1, a minimum security unit filled with hard-core convicts—placed there by unwary corrections officials while renovations at the maximum security cell block were underway.

At last, the long-awaited chance to enact the scheme they had planned . . . conceived with quiet hate and anger. A plan to take command of the penitentiary.

Fortified with liquor and homemade knives, they overpowered the officers on duty, sadistically beating them, sodomizing, torturing. But the brutality suffered by the guards would later seem almost humane compared to the horrors the rioting prisoners were to inflict upon each other.

*   *   *

1:30 p.m., Sunday: Thirty-three inmates dead . . . *all* at the hands of their fellow convicts. Some had been blow-torched to death, others beaten or stabbed . . . one had been beheaded.

It was a reign of terror unparalleled in the history of penal institutions, an outbreak of inmate violence unequaled in the annals of prison uprisings.

New Mexico State Penitentiary . . .

THE
HATE FACTORY

I. Hirliman

A DELL BOOK

Published by Paisano Publications, Inc.
Box 1025
Agoura, California 91301

Nationally Distributed by Dell Distributing, Inc.

Copyright © 1982 by Paisano Publications, Inc.

Dell ® TM 681510. Dell Publishing Co., Inc.

ISBN: 0-440-03686-0

Printed in the United States of America
October 1982
10 9 8 7 6 5 4 3

WFH

I

Brutalization begets brutalization, violence begets violence. In Santa Fe we had a system of penology with a mentality that was all punishment. When you take everything away from a human being including his personal dignity, then he has nothing left to lose. He become extremely dangerous.

—DR. JOHN SALAZAR,
former secretary of corrections,
State of New Mexico[1]

Friday, February 1, 1980. There was a full moon that Friday night. I watched it move across the patch of sky framed by the window near my bunk, noticing how it turned the desert surrounding the penitentiary ghost white. I even thought about all the superstitions connected with the full moon and something I'd read recently about a survey proving that crime really did increase every month when the moon was full. I was tuned in but not enough. It didn't cross my mind that the instigators of a long-planned riot would choose this night to put their scheme into action, maybe because I didn't really think of a prison uprising as something criminal; to me it was a righteous and overdue response to years of abuse, mental and physical. All that overdue rage, though, made people go crazier than anyone expected.

11:45 P.M. Eight well-juiced inmates sat around the table in the dayroom of Dormitory E-2. They'd been chugging down a new batch of home-brew, prison booze made of fermented raisins, yeast, sugar, and water, since just after the early evening headcount at 8:30. Angry and loud, they were gripping about conditions.

"Unless somethin's done soon, The Man's gonna have all the white bros locked down in 3. Over half the brotherhood's in there already," a ranking member of the Aryan Brotherhood told the group. Most of the Anglo population, a minority in this Chicano-dominated prison, belonged to his clique.

"It ain't just you guys. There's a lot of homeboys in lockup right now too," said a lieutenant of the Chicano clique. There was occasional racial tension between the Anglos (the name given to whites in New Mexico) and Chicanos, but usually the two maintained a truce and banned together to fight the blacks, none of whom lived in this dormitory.

"So what are we gonna do about it?" another broke in. "We've been talkin' about a riot for so long now— I'm fuckin' tired of waitin'."

"Okay. What about tonight?"

The eight men sat stunned for a moment, then, nodding agreement, grins spread across their faces.

"Well, *all right,* that's what I want to hear!"

They poured another round of brew, toasted their decision, and began discussing the details of the takeover.

A Chicano leader spoke for his clique. "If we can pull it off, we can count on at least three hundred of our people to back our play. How many white brothers can we count on?"

"At least a hundred and fifty, maybe more. If we can take Cellblock 3, there's another sixty in there."

"I don't trust the blacks. What do you guys think?"

"They're either with us or against us. If they won't go along, we'll fuck them up. But I think they will. They're as tired of The Man's action as we are. In fact, I don't think we're gonna have any trouble gettin' the majority of the population to go along with us."

"Okay, let's get the show on the road, then. We'll take them when they come in for the one-thirty count like we planned. I'll call the white brothers in here, you go get your guys," he addressed the Chicanos at the table. "We'll clue everyone in together. If anyone's asleep, wake the fucker up."

Minutes later, all sixty-two residents of Dormitory E-2 were crowded into the dayroom, the area usually used for TV watching and card games. These inmates had also been drinking and were well-psyched for the news they heard one of the white leaders announce.

"When the pigs come in tonight to take the count, we're gonna grab them and take over this prison." There was an uproar of approval that the speaker had to quiet. "Here's how it's gonna go down. When the two screws who're countin' get to the back of the dorm, three of us will grab them. Another two will take the pig at the door which'll be easy, since these ass-holes never lock it like they're s'posed to. Everyone else look asleep when they come in, but be ready to cover our action when we need you. I know you're creamin' about it now, but just remember when it comes down, anyone who stays in the sack after the shit hits is in trouble."

1:30 A.M., Saturday, February 2, 1980. Shift Captain Gregoria Roybal and Corrections Officers Michael Schmitt and Ronnie Martinez arrived at E-2 to close down the dayroom and take the final count for the night. Officer Martinez opened the dormitory door and Roybal and Schmitt walked into the unit. Martinez waited outside. Lieutenant Jose Anaya arrived unexpectedly just as Martinez was closing the door. He'd received word that there had been drinking going on earlier and decided to come down to back up his fellow officers in case trouble was brewing. He followed Captain Roybal and Officer Schmitt inside. Martinez, as expected, did not lock the door behind them; he left it ajar.

Two of the riot planners were lying in wait on bunks in the center of the room by the entrance door, and two others were on the end bunks near the dayroom; all had homemade shanks (knives) within easy reach under pillows or blankets. When they saw three guards instead of the anticipated two, they felt only a moment of panic before one of them whispered to the man in the next bed, "Pass it on: *Everyone* jumps when we make our move. Get ready."

They let Schmitt make it to the dayroom, lock the door, and turn off the dormitory lights. The leaders knew this would be to their advantage. The only illumination in the place would then come from the bathroom. The blue night lights usually used from lockup to daybreak were out of order and had been for over a month in spite of the fact that a guard had written a memo requesting they be fixed for security reasons. Each time the officers came into this unit for the final count, they became tense. Rumors of a riot had reached the administration's ears back in mid-January, and its promoters were known to be in E-2. Even if a riot hadn't been in the wind, corrections officers would have had reason to be wary. E-2 was a minimum security unit, but just before Thanksgiving it was filled with the most hardcore convicts in the penitentiary. They'd been transferred from Cellblock 5—where the violent, escape-prone, high security-risk inmates were permanently housed—so that renovations could be made in the cellblock. It was doubly eerie for the guards to walk down the long aisles when it was so dark since the officer on watch outside couldn't distinguish the other guards from the inmates by the time the dayroom was reached. The unit was a mine field of double bunks jutting out from both walls and single beds taking up two rows in the center. They knew how easy it would be for an inmate to hide behind one of the double bunks and jump them.

Schmitt came out of the dayroom, and Captain Roybal was halfway down the right aisle while Lieutenant Anaya was four or five bunks in. At that moment all their fears came true. One of the inmates in front sprang from his bed and pushed open the front door while another lunged at Officer Martinez outside, who was struggling to force the door shut. Two men in the back of the dormitory took on Schmitt, and groups in the middle seized Captain Roybal and Lieutenant Anaya. They were all easily overpowered. Captain Roybal and Lieutenant Anaya were both fifty-two years old, short, and not particularly physically fit. The convicts were younger and quicker, and most of them spent a lot of time lifting weights. Only Officer Schmitt had the youth and size to be a challenge, but the sheer number of his opposition brought him down.

The four were dragged into the dayroom, stripped naked, their ankles bound with torn bedsheets, and their hands tied behind their backs.

"Blindfold 'em, too," someone yelled, fastening a canteen-issued bandana tightly around one of the hostage's eyes. "Let's keep these sorry motherfuckers shittin' in their pants—they won't be able t'see nothin', they won't be able to protect themselves. It'll be just like sittin' in the goddamn Hole, hey, pigface? Just like all those times you wrote up tickets on me and sent me into that black pisshole in the basement. Well, it's your turn now, cocksucker."

Using this long-imagined opportunity to pay back The Man, they took turns kicking, punching, spitting, stomping on hands and feet, even pissing on each of the guards, and taunting them with obscenities and threats on their lives and families.

While these beatings were in progress, one of the riot leaders put on Captain Roybal's uniform and, with about ten inmates, went to find the other four officers they knew were working the south side of the penitentiary. Everyone in this group had a weapon of some kind: pipes or shafts smuggled from various prison shops, then stashed in one of the many ingenious hiding places convicts managed to contrive during their abundant idle time. They went downstairs (E-2 is a second-story unit), pushed open the unlocked riot control grill, and stealthily walked the main corridor until they reached the next two dormitories, which were opposite each other.

Seeing no guards in them, they headed upstairs to the top tiers and found what they were after. Officers Elton "Bigfoot" Curry, Juan Bustos, Victor Gallegos, and Herman Gallegos (these two were not related) had just locked down A-2 and were about to enter the dormitory across the hall when the rioters came up from behind and grabbed them. Bustos and Victor Gallegos were easily overpowered, but Curry (nicknamed "Bigfoot" for his size) put up a fight, knocking down several inmates before someone stopped him by stabbing him in the ribs and back. The convicts now had three of the guards under their control. The fourth, Herman Gallegos, had managed to run into the still-unlocked dormitory dayroom. In their hurry to secure their captives, the men didn't go after the officer but counted on the residents of the unit to take care of him. They did, but not the way the rioters expected; Gallegos was lucky enough to find some sympathetic inmates who hid him for the duration of the uprising.

The inmates brought the new hostages down to the E-2 dayroom, stripping, binding, and blindfolding them as they had the first four guards, and throwing them also into the middle of the room to feel the brunt of the prisoners' sadistic violence. It was these seven guards who suffered most at the hands of the rioters mainly because they were captured when the convicts were fresh with unleashed rage. When they looked at their old oppressors lying there naked and helpless, some of them crying in fear, the memories of the maltreatment these same men had forced on them through the years flashed through their minds. Not every one of the seven had been overtly abusive in carrying out his duties, but three of them had.

One specialized in finding subtle ways to play with a man's mind. A favorite stunt was to hold back an inmate's mail for a couple of hours. Before he'd deliver it, he'd read it and then come down to tell the dude what was in the letter. This would infuriate the con, especially when it was from his old lady and was filled with personal sentiments that gave him comfort when read privately but sounded embarrassingly asinine coming out of the guard's snide mouth. This officer was also part of the administration's "goon guard," that group called upon to beat an unruly inmate into submission before he was thrown into The Hole. This was also the main gripe against the other two. Many of the hardcore inmates in this group of rioters could remember days of pain in their lower backs and kidneys caused by the billyclubs of these three guards. They'd never forget being taken to The Hole, hands cuffed to the bars behind them while they were throttled in the kidneys. That's how the goon squad worked—by hitting them in the kidneys and back because the marks there didn't show. These were the guards they sodomized. Using their cocks like weapons, they paid back The Man with the worst humiliation they knew. They did it in "trains," four or five inmates lining up in front of each of the three, coming quickly, as if their semen were bullets. They worked up to such a frenzy that eventually their cocks wouldn't do. They had to take a two-foot billyclub, grease it down (only because they tried it dry and couldn't get it in), and shove it as high as they could up one guard's anus. But they didn't kill them: Dead guards don't talk about the horrors of payback. They wanted these men to live with what had been done to them; they wanted to inflict the same kind of suffering the officers had inflicted on them, the kind they lived with day by day. And they had the sense to remember that live hostages gave them bargaining power.

When this orgy wound down, the riot leader, wearing the Captain's uniform, went with a few inmates to unlock the other dormitories on the south side, which was now in their control. Using the keys taken from the captured guards, the men unlocked the grills to both tiers of each unit, announcing as they entered, "Okay, loosen up, this is a riot. The white bros and Chicanos from E-2 have taken hostage all the screws on this end of the joint. We're gonna take the rest of the place, too. It's time we stood up for ourselves, time to pay back The Man for all the shit he's been givin' us. We're in charge now, not the pigs, so let's go!"

Within fifteen minutes some five hundred inmates were turned loose on the south side of the penitentiary. They armed themselves with legs broken off metal tables and beds, knives, razors, broken jars, locks strung on belts, anything they could use as weapons, tearing the dormitories apart in the process. Only two units on that side were still filled with inmates, one being Dormitory D for which the captured guards had no keys. The men in E-1, a semi-protection unit for the younger men other convicts had tried to rape, turned down their freedom and barricaded themselves in the dormitory with chairs, tables, and beds rammed against the steel door. They had the right idea. The beatings the first seven guards took would seem humane compared to the sadism the rioters would act out in the next thirty-six hours. This was destined to become the most savage prison riot in America's history.

II

So we're all even, right? I did it, I'm here for doing it. Fair and square, no complaint. Paying my debt to The Man. But brother, you got to understand that's just the way it ought to be, that's not the way it is. That Man is committing crimes against me every day I'm here. And nobody's saying shit about that.

INMATE, ATTICA STATE PRISON¹

Why does a person become bitter when they're in prison? How can you avoid it, when the people running the show have nothing in mind but punishing you; when there's no sign of humanity or intelligence shown by those whose job it is to "rehabilitate" you; when society refuses to pay attention to what goes on inside the institutions it shoves its aberrants into; when politicians refuse to allot to such an unpopular cause the money needed to hire adequately educated personnel? And the roots of the bitterness aren't cut off when a convict gets out of prison on parole, either, at least not in New Mexico, "Land of Enchantment."

They've enchanted themselves into believing that a parole officer can take on a caseload of 150 parolees and give the individual supervision needed to help the ex-convict readjust to life on the streets without returning to his old criminal ways. The parole officer does the best he or she can, which isn't very "best" at all. "Stay out of trouble, see me once a month, and make out your report," my parole officer told me. "If you're busted, you go back to prison." In short, don't make any waves for me and I won't make any for you.

I made waves. That's how I ended up back in the joint two months before the February riot, not because I'd been a badass and gone back to my life of crime, but because I'd gotten busted on a bum rap. What mattered to my P.O. wasn't that I was cleared of the beef, or that I was holding down a good job and thereby demonstrating my desire to "reform" and stay out of trouble; what mattered to her was that I'd made her look bad by getting fingered. In her mind, where there's smoke there's fire, so back you go. Let the parole board decide whether the charges were true or not; she wasn't going to take any responsibility beyond the prejudices she'd formed. Maybe, like my P.O., you figure, bum rap my eye, once a con always a con. That's what most people think; that's why getting a job when you're out on parole is a bitch; very few want to risk hiring an ex-felon. So what's he going to do? He's still got to eat, he's still got to find some goodies in life; he's out of money, his P.O., who theoretically is supposed to help him through this difficult transition, is too busy to care. Naturally, he turns to his only friends, ex- or soon-to-be-cons, and the only livelihood he knows. *Whammo*, he's back in the clink.

I was lucky. I had a job, a good job. The halfway

house I'd been paroled to hired me as the maintenance man for $250 a week. My P.O. was all for me for the first four months. Every time I'd go in to see her, she'd tell me how well she thought I was doing. She knew that some of the ex-cons who'd also been paroled to the halfway house worked for me, which meant I was technically violating one of the sacred clauses of the parole contract: no association with ex-felons.

One night I did a co-worker—an ex-con—a favor and drove him to a friend's house. His friend wasn't there, but the girl who answered the door said she'd show us where to find him. We drove around with the girl for a few hours, stopping at several places but never locating the dude. Finally, at about 1:00 in the morning, we gave up and took the girl home. As luck would have it, her mother met us at the door, in a rage that her daughter had been out so late: The girl was not the twenty-year-old she looked to be but a jailbait fifteen. We were happy to drive away from this scene, but the next day we found out there was more to come. To cover her action, the fifteen-year-old told her mother we'd raped her, and mother and daughter had traipsed down to the Rape Crisis Center the following morning to tell the tale. A warrant was issued for our arrest. When I heard about it, I turned myself in to show that I had nothing to hide. When I explained to my parole officer that there was nothing to the charge, that I was innocent, she said, "If you can beat the rap, I'll release you." I breathed a little easier as I sat stewing in the county jail waiting for the grand jury to hear the evidence against me. When they did, a month later, there was no evidence. The girl had not only left town, but the medical report showed that she hadn't had sexual intercourse for at least forty-eight hours prior to the time she'd been tested. The grand jury refused to indict me, and the rape charge was thrown out. I beat the rap, but my P.O. had changed her mind about releasing me. She couldn't keep me locked up on the original charge because it had been dropped, but she found a new one that would automatically revoke my parole: associating with an ex-felon, a horseshit charge if I ever heard one, given the fact that she knew all along I was working side by side with parolees. Did she expect me not to be sociable with them, to turn down a request for a favor as simple as driving the ex-con somewhere? Frankly, I think the word *rape* freaked her out.

Believe it or not, I'm all for equality for women, but I don't see the point in having a young, inexperienced female counselling a forty-year-old man who's spent the last fourteen years behind bars relating only to hardened male criminals. I hadn't been near a woman in so long I hardly knew how to act with them when I got out. How in the hell was I supposed to go to her with the problems I was going through: for instance, the impotence that hit me for the first two months after my release, not an uncommon complaint for male parolees. And in fairness to her, how was she supposed to understand where I was coming from? To her, I was a dangerous criminal, and the smoke of the rape charge meant fire to her.

She told my old lady, who'd gone in to plead my case, that she believed I'd done it in spite of the proof to the contrary. "He should be locked up; he'd be better off in prison. He'd be away from society and society would be protected," she'd said. But that wasn't all she revealed about the nature of her prejudices (and how she could be so stupid as to reveal these things to anyone is just another mark of the inadequacy of the corrections system in this Land of Enchantment). "Two of my clients besides Wally have just been arrested, and it really bothers me that my clients keep breaking the laws like this, making me do extra paper work and giving me these headaches. I got called on the carpet to explain why so many of my clients were doing so poorly; they make me look like I'm not doing my job well." She went on to say that she was afraid of people like me. To her, I was exactly like one of her other clients, a man who'd just gotten arrested for raping his wife with a hot curling iron! "Wally's in the same class with him," she wound up. "You might as well kiss him goodbye, because he's going back to the penitentiary where he belongs."

And so I went. I had a preliminary hearing before a hearing officer, but I knew that this officer, also a woman, would act on my P.O.'s recommendation, which she did. Still, this wasn't the final ruling; that decision was reserved for the three-member parole board itself. Until they could find the time to hear my case and rule on whether I was fit to reenter society, however, I had to spend more time in the overcrowded, cockroach-infested penitentiary where I'd already lost fourteen years of my life.

It was a cold, cloudy December Monday when I walked through the prison gates, and my mood was as dark as the weather. The street clothes I was just getting used to wearing were taken from me by the admitting officer and put in an envelope; in their place I was given the drab green prison uniform I'd worn for so many years. I was assigned to the "old men's dormitory," where the old-timers who couldn't cope with the madness of the general population lived along with guys like me who were either doing short time on parole violations or waiting for a hearing. Like every other unit in the institution, C-1 was overcrowded. Built to house forty inmates, I was the forty-eighth. There were no more single beds available, so I was assigned an upper bunk. I'd gotten spoiled in my six months out; I was used to sleeping on a firm bed. This one tore me apart. Even in the county jail the mattress hadn't been so thin. I could feel the metal springs of the frame, and they sagged so that my spine ached after my first night's sleep, what little of it I was able to get.

During the next few days I found out that my own anger at being back in this hellhole, especially since I'd done nothing to deserve it, matched the resentment that was seething in my old friends. My fellow inmates were ready to move against The Man; in fact, they'd planned to grab hostages and take over the place just before I arrived, but a snitch had gotten wind of the details and told the administration, so the scheme was postponed. It wasn't called off, however. Things were too oppressive in the penitentiary for the men to forget about making their troubles known, and making them known was the major purpose of the overthrow they were planning. They knew that only riots made Johnny Q. Public think about conditions behind the walls; that only through violent protest would prison authorities make even the smallest commitment to better those conditions. Racial prejudices were set aside so there would be unanimity during the takeover, at least among the Chicanos and whites. Tension between blacks and the Chicano and white cliques was too high for any sit-down discussions among them to be practical. Since there were less than 200 blacks among the 1,156 men in the prison, their advice and consent didn't seem important to the planning of the riot. But plenty of secret meetings were going on between the Aryan Brotherhood and the Mexican Mafia.

It was from a white bro I'd known during my last five years in the joint that I learned the details of the takeover. I knew his information was reliable because he was one of the lieutenants in the Aryan Brotherhood. First, though, I had to listen to his gripes.

"I don't know how long the white brothers can maintain and keep cool," he told me, "because The Man is always fuckin' us over. If one of us has a good job, he moves him to another one. Some of the brothers have been tryin' to enter the educational department and take some courses, to try for once to show somethin' for the time they're doin', but the cocksucker always gives us some bullshit excuse about why he won't let us in. Last time one of the bros was told he couldn't get in because there are too many female teachers: 'You guys are bikers and too dangerous for us to let loose with the women!' What the fuck does he think we're gonna do, eat the broads out in front of the goddamn guards?" We both got a laugh out of that; it's been known to happen. "That fuckass Deputy Warden Montoya, all you have to do to get on his wrong side is have a goddamned Harley Davidson tatoo; I swear he hates bikers more than he hates whites. He dishes out more crap to us brothers, as if it wasn't bad enough in this cesspool without him playin' his power trips on us.

"The thing that's gettin' to everyone, whites, niggers, Mexicans alike, is that this place is gettin' so fucking overcrowded there's almost no room to breathe. Everywhere you turn, somebody's there. Their feet stink, there's about six inches between you and the dude in the bed next to you, and you can't even move your arm over without hittin' someone in the face. Here's eighty-five guys crammed into a dorm built to hold fifty; some cells have two dudes in them now, so there goes *all* hope of privacy, locked in there with some asshole you might feel like pissin' on. It's impossible to have any quiet, with radios tuned to every station in the state turned up to full volume. You try to sleep or read or even jerk off to some fine fantasy, but you can't, and you can't get away cause there ain't no place to go, not one place in this whole friggin' joint where you can go be alone so maybe you can snivel to yourself about how bad you feel instead of punchin' someone out to relieve it. And of course, there's always the fuckin' food to complain about, as if there wasn't enough already. You know, just a week ago they served us rotten turkey, so help me God, smelling, green, rotten turkey. About four hundred guys got the shits, but The Man just shrugged it off like it was nothin'. Have you noticed the guards?"

I told him I had, that they hadn't changed since I'd left six months ago.

"No, man, they're worse, and they get worse every shit-eatin' day. There's a slew of these new ones, and they're the worst motherfuckers I've ever seen, all in their early twenties; one's only eighteen, and none of them have any training except in how to carry a chip on their shoulder and a bad attitude. Here's some eighteen-year-old punk thinks he's hot shit 'cause he's wearin' a uniform and carryin' a club, been on the job four months and he walks up to a forty-five-year-old lifer and orders him around like he's some dumb dog.

Just the age alone is enough t'make the con resent the screw, let alone the way the sonofabitch talks down to him. I tell you, bro, we've had it—we're gonna put a stop to it. We had it all planned, but a snivellin' snitch squelched it—but we're gonna roll again, when the time's right."

My friend was a tatooed bonafide biker from California who believed in white power to the max: His white brothers came before anybody or anything; right or wrong, he covered their action. He was known by inmates and administration alike as one of the prison's hardcore troublemakers. He came in on a two-to-ten-year term for forgery but earned another two-to-ten for manslaughter by taking part in a penitentiary murder a few years back along with two of his tight white brothers. He usually lived in Cellblock 5 with the other "incorrigibles," but in November they'd all been moved from that maximum security cellblock to the minimum security Dormitory E-2. Though the transfer had been made to turn 5 into a more secure unit with electronically locked doors, it astounded many corrections officers as much as it pleased the sixty troublemakers who'd been relocated. It was after this transfer that riot rumbles began, all emanating from E-2.

The original plan had revolved around a show that the local university radio station, KUNM, was going to broadcast from the prison gymnasium the first Saturday in December. The inmates were going to take the deejays hostage, along with the guards assigned to the area, and use the broadcasting facilities to communicate to KUNM's large listening audience what conditions were like in the penitentiary and what demands would have to be met before the hostages were freed. When the administration got word of the takeover from the informer, they advised the station of the plan and cancelled the show. The deejays who'd set up the event didn't trust the prison authorities to be straight with them, however, since the prison's long-standing dislike of the media was well-known. The deejays wrote to their inmate contact, naïvely asking them if what they'd heard about a riot plan was true. The cons replied quite naturally, "Who, us? No, the administration just doesn't want you in here; they're trying to cover up as usual, afraid people might hear or see something that's going to hurt them and bust their precious bubble." Media people being the trouble-shooters of the world, the station management started making a lot of noise about their right of access and finally got permission to do a broadcast from the inside of the penitentiary in April or May of 1980, the exact date to be chosen later.

Some riot leaders decided they'd bide their time until then, since the show offered them such good access to hostages and broadcasting facilities. But others involved in the planning were not so patient. There was a faction of the Aryan Brotherhood, together with a few Chicanos, that had been talking about an escape since the middle of November, when Cellblock 5 was transferred to E-2, but they'd put it off when there seemed to be a chance to take over the prison. Taking over the institution had been this group's first preference anyway, with a few variations on the theme. Their idea was to get fifty mostly white brothers into the gym with twenty to forty blacks who they'd stab to death (you don't need a reason to hate in prison—rage is so abundant you just need a scapegoat to act out on); when the slaughter was over, they'd take the hospital and psychological units, hold the guards hostage, and shoot up, drink, or swallow all the drugs they could find. However, this idea was cancelled as being too impractical, and the group went with an escape plan instead. When the riot didn't come down, they decided to go for it.

There were eleven inmates in on the deal. On Saturday night, December 8, one of them took a smuggled hacksaw blade and cut through the steel grillwork in his cell window while another kept watch across the hall. The next night, December 9, after the big Sunday dinner, thirty residents of Cellhouse 2, where the escape was to be staged, congregated in the back of the mess hall and surrounded six men from the other cellblocks who were in on the escape, walking them past the guard on duty in Cellhouse 2. This wasn't difficult to do, since the officers rarely knew exactly who lived in which unit. All eleven inmates jammed into the six-by-nine-foot cell where the hole had been cut in the window. When they were sure the guard in the tower nearest them was asleep, they climbed out, one by one. They'd been watching this tower guard for weeks and knew that he regularly slept on the job. (All convicts knew that tower duty was the shit shift, so boring that the screws made a practice of using the time to catch up on their sleep. This was the second escape in two years accomplished right under the nose of a sleeping tower guard.) These eleven men made it across a brightly lit lawn and cut a hole in a part of the perimeter fence that was directly in the shadow of the tower.

That guard was fired when the escape was finally discovered. He was in his early twenties, had been at the institution for only a year, and, like most of the new officers, had far too little training in the realities he was likely to encounter working in a maximum-security prison. His failure on duty wasn't all his fault, though. According to security regulations, the control center and all the guard towers are supposed to be in telephone communication with each other every half-hour. If a tower didn't call in, the control center was supposed to phone him to be sure the dude was awake, a built-in precaution for the boring nature of tower duty. Both the cellhouse guard and the supervisor for the night were given thirty-day suspensions for not paying attention to their jobs, but these slaps on the hand didn't begin to touch the problems caused by untrained personnel and the laxness of security in the joint. Things were definitely unravelling in New Mexico's penitentiary.

A year before the escape, a former California corrections official did a study of the institution for the American Justice Institute; in that study he called the prison "one of the most poorly administered he'd ever encountered."[2] Still, nothing had been done to upgrade the management. The New Mexico Attorney General investigated conditions in the penitentiary after the December 9 escape and told the public in his report what every inmate in the prison knew: that it had "a history of instability and poor planning"; that management was rampant with "factionalism, poor communication, and apathy"; that one of the worst problems was "the volatile condition of overcrowding and misuse of dormitories for medium security prisoners . . . We cannot afford to wait for another major incident and hope again that our resources and planning will come together before the situation becomes critical." He concluded that by staffing the institution with guards who were recent high-school graduates with no training for prison work, the state's officials were "playing Russian roulette with the lives of inmates, staff, and the public."

Like I said, only a riot turns the bureaucrat's head around. This report, issued less than a month before the Russian roulette broke out on February 2, made no impression on prison officials, at least none they acted on. In spite of these findings, in spite of warnings from informers that riot plans were still in the air, that weapons were being stashed in Dormitory E-2, that the leaders of the riot were also in this dormitory, the administration did nothing to tighten security. They held a lot of meetings to discuss the information and once sent a team in to search E-2, but nothing was found though plenty was there.

The institution was being run so sloppily that the riot instigators began to wonder if The Man was daring them to start something. The riot control grills separating each dormitory from the main corridor of the prison hadn't been locked for the past six months. Even though these gates, like so much in the place, were being renovated to allow their electronic operation from the control center, guards were supposed to lock them manually every night. But they weren't doing it. Later they'd tell investigators that it was "too cumbersome" to do so; and the administration would say they felt no urgency about getting the grills hooked up electronically, though they could have gotten the job done in a matter of days. In addition to these grills to the individual dormitories, there were two riot control gates that separated both the north and south sides of the penitentiary from the control center. These were supposed to be locked every day at 4:30 P.M., after daily activities were finished, but they, too, were being left open at night.

When "shatterproof" glass was installed in the

wraparound windows of the control center, the riot instigators considered it another mark in their favor. They saw weaknesses the prison authorities and legislators who approved the glass obviously didn't. The 3/16-inch-thick, one-way bulletproof pane replaced small windows with steel grillwork that had been found to "inhibit effective monitoring" and to cause "blind spots which cannot be seen from the central control area." Betting it could be broken easily, the riot leaders counted the destruction of the new glass as one of their first attack priorities.

On January 6, a relatively minor racial incident bloomed into a situation that fired a move to set the riot in motion sooner than planned. A fight broke out in Cellhouse 2 between Ronnie Stout, a white bro, and a black professional boxer. The boxer whipped Stout's ass and gave him two purple eyes. This angered the white clique. Ronnie Stout was a heavy in the prison. He'd done a lot of time and was about to get out on parole. He also had a twin brother, Donnie, who'd done an equal number of years in the joint and had just come back on a new twelve-to-sixty-year sentence for armed robbery. They'd always had an exceptional bond with each other, so much so that they pulled their robberies together and sometimes used their resemblance to trade off punishments. They talked a lot about a psychic connection they thought they had with each other. As Ronnie described it, "I'd know something was wrong with Donnie and I'd get up and go wherever he was; no one could stop me when I felt it."[3] Donnie heard about the fight, probably more from the grapevine than ESP, and he was ready to jump to Ronnie's aid. He got members of the Aryan Brotherhood to go down to Ronnie's cell the next morning to discuss what kind of payback they should lay on the black who was responsible for the beating, but Ronnie told the group he didn't want any trouble. He'd made his parole and was due to get out at the end of the month; a fight on his behalf would only fuck up his chance for freedom. Donnie and the white brothers agreed to forget about the whole incident, and a race war was averted.

Deputy Warden Robert Montoya, however, had gotten word of the fight and the powwow about retribution. That afternoon he had Donnie Stout and his fifteen henchmen, along with the black, locked up in Cellblock 3, the segregation unit, on the charge that they were plotting a race riot. Prison rules and regulations state that no inmate is to be kept in lockup under investigation of a charge for more than five days. At the end of five days he has to be found guilty of the charge or set free. The prison's intelligence officer, Eugene Morgan, turned in a report to Montoya that stated the fight between Stout and the black was personal rather than racial, that nothing further would happen once the men were released from segregation. But Montoya didn't release them. In spite of the findings and in spite of prison policy, he kept the men in lockup for sixteen more days. If one of the inmates hadn't gotten a letter through to the Civil Liberties Union, they might have been there longer. As it was, an attorney called the warden and warned him that if the men weren't released from Cellblock 3, the issue would be settled through the courts. Only then were they returned to population.

Because Montoya had been creating episodes like this for the past five years, he'd become the most hated administrator in the institution. With this incident he exhibited extreme bad timing; it was the drop of water that drove the prisoner crazy. The riot leaders conferred and resolved that they'd move at the first opportunity. They thought they'd pick a Monday because there'd be more civilians around in the offices to take as hostage, but they weren't setting any dates; they'd play it by ear, and everyone would have to be ready in a moment's notice. From then on, the instigators in E-2 spent their free time psyching themselves up for war.

I laid on my upper bunk that last night in January, somewhere between crying and pounding on the wall. The board members had granted me parole, but some sadistic twist in their natures made them choose April 23 as my release date. I knew I was going to get stuck in this riot; my friends weren't about to wait two weeks, no less two months, to start it. I had no taste for an uprising. I just wanted to get out of the place and never see it again, outside or inside, and I didn't want anything messing up my chance to do just that. This put me between a rock and a hard spot. If I got into it, like part of me wouldn't mind doing for the sake of payback, The Man could revoke my parole and send me up on new charges. If I didn't participate in the festivities, I could get my throat cut. I'd been there long enough to know that you're either with a convict or against him and that the choice means life or death; there's no middle ground. Yet the middle ground was exactly what I was going to have to find. The more I thought about it, the more depressed I got. Why in the hell had the parole board made me wait? The question kept running through my head all night even though I knew the answer as well as my name: because they just don't give a damn about the lives they have such control over; because they don't think of convicts as human beings, they think of us as animals. And by God, don't we become them. By the time daybreak came I'd imagined myself smashing in the heads of every parole person who'd put me in this predicament.

III

One cannot endure a penalty so monstrous as the lack of freedom without demanding of one's mind and body a labor at once delicate and brutal, a labor capable of warping the prisoner in a direction which takes him ever farther from the social world.

JEAN GENET[1]

2:00 A.M., Saturday, February 2, 1980. I was sitting on my bed talking to the guy in the next bunk when we were interrupted by the sound of yelling and screaming. My first thought was that The Man was taking some out-of-line inmates to lockup. Cellblock 3, the segregation unit, was just down the hall from me, and while it was a daily occurrence for a guard to be dragging a troublemaker through the corridor past my dorm, and it was equally as common for the screw to be smacking the con in the ribs with his stick all the way, these cries were stronger than usual, and got my curiosity up. I jumped down from my bunk and walked into the shower room to check it out through a window

29

overlooking the control center and the main corridor. I saw screaming inmates alright—seventy-five to one hundred of them running from the south end up to the control center booth, waving all kinds of makeshift weapons. Those in the front of this mob were dragging a barely crawling, naked, blindfolded man by a belt looped around his neck. Those behind were kicking him in the ribs and ass and wacking him in the legs, which, like his arms, were tied; I saw someone bring a chain down hard across his back and the man crumbled, but the crowd was determined to keep him moving. They kicked him more viciously in the butt, whipping him with their pipes while the one holding the "leash" yanked it hard, until finally the hostage got back on his hands and knees and resumed his painful crawl.

"Unlock the gate or we'll beat the shit out of your friend here," the rioter holding the belt demanded of the guard inside the booth who couldn't be seen through the mirrored window.

That officer, Lawrence Lucero, had ordered the guards on the north side to lock the north grill just minutes earlier after hearing one of the riot leaders announce over a confiscated two-way radio that they'd taken over the prison, were holding seven guards hostage, and wanted a meeting set up with the Governor, the news media, and the Deputy Secretary of Corrections. Lucero immediately phoned the chief of security, Emanuel Koroneos, at his home and advised him that a riot was in progress. At the same time, Louis C de Baca, one of the guards on foot patrol outside the building, heard over his radio the dialogue between Lucero and the inmate and ran into the penitentiary to help his co-workers, remembering that renovations then in progress on the electronic systems would make it difficult for Lucero to get out of the control booth alone. While the door wasn't operating electrically, the only way it could be opened from the inside was by reaching through the bars of the door with key in hand and blindly attempting to fit it in the lock. If this guard hadn't been on the ball, the officer inside the booth would have been cursing the inefficiency of the administration as he realized he wasn't going to be able to get the door open and get out. C de Baca made it into the control center just as the rioters reached it from the outside and made their demand for the grill to be opened.

"Unlock the gate, motherfucker, or you're gonna have one dead screw on your hands," the rioter repeated.

"No way," Officer Lucero replied from inside. He wasn't able to open the north grill anyway, since it wasn't electronically connected to the control panel, but the gate to the administrative offices behind him was. In refusing the inmate's demand, Lucero was following the officers' code not to give in to threats by inmates. He had to bear the consequences of heeding the code by watching the rioters attack their naked hostage, a twenty-five-year-old guard who'd worked at the penitentiary for only a year, until they'd drawn blood with the pipes, metal table legs, chains, and homemade knives they beat him with. They stopped then to see if Lucero had changed his mind, but he hadn't, and the convicts again surged around their kneeling victim, kicking, punching, and pounding him with their weapons until he fell unconscious. Maybe they let up then because he looked like he was dead; Lucero would later say he thought they'd killed him.

"See what you've done now?" someone yelled in at Lucero. "If you don't open up, it's gonna be you next, suckface."

But the officer wouldn't give in.

While a small group dragged the unconscious guard's body back to the south end, the bulk of the rioters started beating on the control center's new shatterproof window with their pipes. A mop bucket was hurled at it several times, and finally someone grabbed a fire extinguisher off the wall and hurled it against the glass. On the third throw the safety window began cracking. Shatterproof indeed! As slivers began splintering inside the control center, the two guards realized the booth was vulnerable and panicked. Instead of attempting to stop the rioters by flooding the place with tear gas stored in the booth for just such emergencies, they ran out, not thinking to take with them the keys to the rest of the institution which were hanging on the key board. Lucero, twenty-four years old with three years experience in the penitentiary, and C de Baca, twenty-two, with only one year, ran out of the prison's front entrance into the safety of the main tower. They were the first officers to escape the riot.

Inside, five minutes after the rioters began their attack on the control center, the newly installed, bulletproof glass had a gaping hole in it and the inmates were in command of the nerve center of the institution, with access to practically every unit. Seven or eight of them pulled the glass loose and stepped through the open window into the booth, demolishing everything in sight, opening the trap door that led to the compartment where all the riot gear was kept, and handing out tear gas guns and bombs, batons, riot helmets, and gas

masks. It was a bizarre scene, like some celebration of
D-Day in a POW camp. As the weapons came up, the
crowd grabbed them, waving them in the air, putting
on gas masks and helmets. Someone accidently fired
one of the tear gas guns, filling the corridor with as-
phyxiating smoke and fumes; this sent the mob into fits
of choking and gasping but didn't drain them of their
excitement. They were wild with their new-found
power, jumping up and down in a raging jig, shouting:

"Let's go get the snitches. . . ."

"Burn the fuckin' records, man, let's go!"

"Let's hit the pharmacy and find us some reds!"

It was bedlam, the shouting turning into a roaring
wave of war cries and curses. Inside the control booth,
a Chicano rioter was unrolling the folded American
flag put there every night for safekeeping. "Hey, man,
don't you think this would make a fine poncho?" he
asked the Anglo next to him who laughed in response
and continued going through the desk drawers. The
Chicano took a pair of scissors, cut a hole in the middle of the flag, and slipped it over his head. Later he
would become one of the main negotiators, talking
over the two-way radio, wearing his American flag
poncho until it got too bloody to be comfortable.

The original seventy-five rioters who'd stormed the
control center had increased in number as the other
freed inmates from the south side joined them. A large
group invaded the administration offices behind the
control booth and began tearing them apart, going
through desks and filing cabinets, throwing everything
inside them into piles in the middle of the office floors
and setting them on fire, burning every record of every
convict in the penitentiary. They went through the
I.D. office in the basement of the institution, where the

private property, including money, of newly arrived inmates was kept. Some lucky dude found approximately $1200 in there, money that was never recorded and is probably still floating around the penitentiary's underground stashes, if it hasn't already been used to purchase smack, grass, or L.S.D. or to cover gambling debts. They had access to phones and used them well, calling wives, relatives, and friends all over the United States. People in Canada and New York knew there was a riot going on in New Mexico before downtown Santa Fe, eleven miles away, knew about it. Their friends cheered them on, told them, "More power to you"— words these friends would later regret when the power became barbaric. But at this early point in the uprising just about every inmate in the prison, myself included, was silently congratulating the rioters for pulling it off; some of the snitches in Cellblock 4 probably were, too. The freeing of bonds is always exhilarating, at least in the beginning.

While this bunch was assaulting the control center and the administrative offices, totally demolishing everything in sight, another group had opened the north grill and was running through the main corridor on the north side shouting, "This is a riot, let's go!" They opened Cellblock 6 and the old men's dormitory where I was, but when the leaders went to get their friends out of Cellblock 3, Segregation, they found they hadn't taken the right keys from the control center. A few went back to find them while others stormed up to the grill separating the snitches in Cellblock 4 from the corridor and taunted them with threats. "Breathe your last breaths, motherfuckers, 'cause you've only got a little while to live. When we get the keys to this grill, here, you suckers are gonna pay. . . ." They wouldn't be able to find the keys to the grill, and its electronic operation, though working, was jammed, so the snitches had plenty of time to barricade their cells, though they didn't know it. For them, the next few hours were ones of grim expectation.

There were fifteen guards on duty inside the prison, less than half, it was later determined, than the number working at other similarly overcrowded prisons across the nation; this in spite of the fact that the Penitentiary of New Mexico was known to be primed for an imminent explosion. Seven of these guards, including the shift commander, Captain Roybal, had been taken hostage on the south side; one was being hidden by sympathetic inmates in Dormitory F-1; Officer Mike Hernandez, assigned to Dormitory D-1, had locked himself into the educational unit, which, along with D-1, was closed off from the rest of the institution by a corridor grill; Officer Lucero, on duty in the control center, had run out of the prison. This left five more officers, all of them on the north end of the building, for the inmates to deal with, plus one civilian, the hospital technician. When the rioters gained access to the control center, these six staff members began to seek safety from the mob they knew would soon break through the north security grill. The officer assigned to Cellhouse 6, Antonio Vigil, who'd worked at the penitentiary for twenty-two years, and Valentin Martinez, a ten-year veteran who was assigned this night to Cellblock 4, where the snitches lived, phoned the guard on duty outside in Tower 3 and informed him they'd be hiding in the basement crawl space near the gas chamber. They warned him not to transmit their hiding place over the two-way radios for fear the inmates would pick up the information. They'd chosen a good spot, remaining hidden and unharmed for the duration of the uprising. The infirmary technician, Ross Maez, another old-timer with twenty-two years at the prison, locked himself in a small room at the far end of the upstairs section of the hospital along with seven inmate patients. The last three guards, Officers Larry Mendoza, Edward Ortega, and Ramon Gutierrez, all assigned to Cellblock 3, where the hardcore trouble-makers were kept in segregation, locked themselves in the basement area of CB 3. Mendoza and Guiterrez were both young; one had been a guard for three years, the other for only one. Ortega, however, was a twenty-three-year veteran of the institution. Mendoza was one of the more alert officers on duty this night. Realizing he had left the main key to Cellblock 3 in a small box in the vestibule of the middle level, he crawled upstairs and retrieved it. While he was there, the rioters who had just realized they couldn't open the grill saw him and yelled in, "Open the gate, Mendoza, or when we do get it open you're dead." But he refused and returned to the basement, locking himself in with the other two officers in an area used to store bedding.

By now about thirty inmates had entered the hospital unit and had gone straight for the pharmacy and the filing cabinet where they knew all the drugs were kept. They set about prying the cabinet open and in minutes had themselves a candy store of every kind of downer you can think of, from valium to Miltown to reds to codeine, even liquid Demerol, available to all comers in any dosage desired. There were also hypodermic needles and syringes for those who liked a more potent hit. The state had a purchasing policy that required them to buy in bulk, a policy that came in handy for the rioters, or so they thought as they stood there shooting up, swallowing pills, indulging in far more than their systems would eventually be able to handle. They filled up shoeboxes with the colorful capsules and tablets along with bottles of Demerol, syringes, and needles, heaped pills into their pockets, and staggered euphorically back into the hallway to turn on their friends. They never bothered to look upstairs, so the seven people hidden there remained undiscovered until the riot was over. Nor did the rioters lay the unit to waste as they had every other place they'd entered. Their only interest was drugs; once they had them, they unconsciously paid homage to their benefactor.

While these thirty were raiding their candy store, another group was tearing apart the psychological unit. One thing the rioters seemed set on was burning every record in the prison. They dumped all the files into the middle of the floor, along with carpets, wooden chairs, and tables, and set fire to them. This was going to be a big blaze, not like the smaller ones in the administrative offices. They were out to totally destroy the unit.

"Hey you guys, we're burnin' that fucker Orner's headquarters down," they warned those of us in the old men's dorm just above. "Let the bastard see how we feel about him. You're gonna suffocate to death if you don't split. We know lots of you dudes are too old to join with us, some of you got short time before you'll be gettin' home, so maybe you don't want any part of all this shit; and we can dig it, but it looks like you're bein' forced into it regardless, either that or die with the smoke."

I could sympathize with their wanting to get back at the head of the psych unit, Dr. Marc Orner. He was a longtime member of the administration that had run the institution for twenty years and an abuser of the snitch system[2] that had landed just about every con with any balls at all in the hole at least once. None of us felt like leaving the dormitory, though, in spite of the smoke that was beginning to drift up. Between the haze it created and the crazed way these guys looked—half of them like space soldiers with their gas masks and tear gas guns, the other half a throwback to old west outlaws, bandanas pulled up over their faces, wielding pipes and batons like they were rifles—it was like standing at the entrance to hell. Through this entrance came a few barefaced rioters passing around the pill-filled shoeboxes. I refused the offer, but others in the dorm took handfuls, hoping a high would make the craziness easier to handle. I wanted to keep my head straight and clear so I'd get through it all in one piece; this was going to be worse than I'd ever imagined. I'd been watching dudes line up in the corridor just a few minutes before, about twenty of them, queuing up like it was a shooting gallery, waiting their turn to push some Demerol into their veins, then staggering out into the corridor waving their pipes and table legs in the air, whooping and hollering about "killing that asshole that burned me . . . ." Whatever exhilaration I'd felt earlier was gone. As for getting out and walking among these madmen or staying in the dorm and taking our chances with the smoke, we were of one mind: We opted for the smoke.

"Okay, that's your problem, then; don't say we didn't warn you," the gas-masked spokesman for the group told us and walked out with his platoon. They could have slit our throats for not wanting to join them, but this group seemed to understand our stake in not getting involved. We doubted, as the riot progressed, that others would.

IV

If you are a free person that's a racist, if you hate, this is one of the few places where you can come and exercise it with encouragement and impunity. The emphasis of this institution is man's inhumanity against man, and to oppress an inmate at any cost. There's a penalty here for being respectable to an inmate.

INMATE, STATEVILLE PRISON,
Joliet, Illinois[1]

Prison is a jungle where the strong survive, and only the strong. It's not so different from life in that respect, except that a penitentiary is a zoo and the inmates caged animals. They're fed like animals, treated like animals, and encouraged to behave like animals toward one other. The meals are slopped on metal plates just like they are for animals in a zoo. The food itself, basically starch and pork, is geared to keep a human functioning on the dullest animal level. The walls, which are painted a depressing khaki, match the unflattering uniforms inmates must wear. There is nothing in the prison to help a man remember that he is a human being who can evolve out of his past mistakes; everything points to his failure and hammers it into his consciousness. Respect is quickly forgotten; none is shown to convicts by any prison administrator or guard, except the respect won by being the toughest animal and causing fear. I once heard a politician say that the law of survival meant that if you're going to survive you must be king. In the joint, if you have any intentions of surviving, you've got to be the king animal. How you relate to people here is completely different from how you're used to relating on the outside. You can't be nice; nice guys don't last. You quickly find out that kindness is a weakness in the joint. If you tell a guy, "Yeah, I'll loan you a dollar," he'll think: "Look at this weak sonofabitch. He's easy; I'll hit him for fifty dollars next time." Or he'll come back every week for that same dollar or that same candy bar you first offered. It's one big head game that breaks down to the golden rule of survival in the convict jungle: Do unto others before they do it to you.

I arrived at the Penitentiary of New Mexico on a ten-to-fifty-year armed robbery conviction in 1962, twenty-two years old and scared shitless. I'd been prepared for the hard facts of prison life by some parole violators in the county jail who were there with me while I was waiting to be sentenced. They told me that if I was going to make it, I'd have to stand up for myself the first time something came down. And plenty, they said, would come down. The majority of the population at the time was Chicano, some 600 of them, with about 200 blacks and only 100 whites. For the first time in my life I was going to be part of a minority group, an even more vulnerable position in a prison than it is in the outside world. They warned me that when young white guys came into population at Santa Fe (what we called the penitentiary because of its proximity to that city), they'd get hit on for a piece of ass. The new white boy had a choice: stand up for himself or get pushed to the limit for the rest of his time there.

My first month was spent in Quarantine, where all newcomers are kept for thirty days while they're given a battery of physical, mental, and emotional tests before joining the rest of the prison population. Why all this is done I've never understood; the administration certainly never used the results to help rehabilitate anyone, and many men with psychological problems were sent to coexist with the general prison population. Nevertheless, a week after I'd been released from Quarantine, I had a chance to prove what kind of convict I was going to be.

I'd been assigned to a dormitory, a dangerous place for a novice to the prison game. A convict didn't get a cell of his own until he'd done some time and proven he wasn't a troublemaker. Once he'd earned it, he'd be assigned to a cellhouse unit and a "house." He'd be free to move in population for meals and work, but at night he'd have the luxury of a locked cell where nobody could attack him. Then the sound of the metal door snapping shut would be a welcome one. But in the dormitories, when that door clanked every night at lockup, it was time to be on guard. For the first few months that sound sent chills up my spine, but eventually I got used to it. In prison you adjust to closing metal doors or you go crazy. In prison, you adjust to every kind of inhumanity or go berserk. I was sitting on my bunk one Saturday afternoon when a black convict walked up to me.

"Hey, how about helpin' us out?" he said.

I asked him what he meant.

"Well, we've been checkin' you out, and me and a couple buddies of mine decided we wanna fuck your butt. All the white guys that come in here, they all turn around and help out the brothers, and the brothers go ahead and take care of them. We'll take care of you, too; we won't let the Mexicans fuck with you."

I told him I wasn't at all interested.

"Well, if you don't, we'll come over tonight and take it anyway, so you just think about how you want it."

I was a fairly naïve twenty-two-year-old and had never been approached by a man sexually; I also held the racial prejudices that were as normal among white folks in 1962 as apple pie and mom were, so the prospect that stared me in the face was triply offensive. Fortunately I'd made the acquaintance of an old-timer in another unit, and I went to him with my problem. He listened and was typically noncommittal.

"Well, what do you want to do about it?" he asked.

I told him I only knew I didn't want anything to do with the dude and asked what he thought I *should* do about it.

"If you don't stand up to them now, they're gonna go ahead and fuck you and you're gonna end up a jailhouse punk; you'll have a hard way to go that way. I seen a lot of white boys get fucked by the blacks and the Chicanos in the five years I been here; most of them were raped and they all became punks, jailhouse ladies. If you stand up to them, you might get your ass whipped, but when it's all over, they won't bother you no more."

I explained that standing up to them was what I had in mind, but the guy that approached me was big, plus he had a friend, maybe two; how was I going to fight them all and come out alive?

"I got somethin' that'll help you," he told me, stomping out the butt of his Camel. He left his bunk and went into the shower room. When he came back, he handed me a two-foot piece of radiator pipe, which I quickly put down my trousers, holding it against my thigh with one hand. He hadn't sawed off the pipe in that quick trip; he just kept his personal arsenal of weapons stashed somewhere in the lavatory. It was for just such battles that these weapon stashes were kept by most of the hardcore cons.

That night, I laid on top of my bunk waiting, the pipe by my side. At about 1:30 in the morning, I saw my would-be attacker walking up the aisle toward me. I tensed and took a deep breath. He approached my bed and whispered.

"Hey, you ready, boy?"

I told him, yeah, I was ready.

"Okay," he said in a satisfied low voice. "Let's go to the dayroom; we got something for you you're gonna love."

I got up and he started walking in front of me. I thought to myself, I got something for you, too, sucker. He didn't quite get to turn around before I slammed the pipe against the side of his head. He didn't go down, just stood there like he was in shock, his eyes wide, staring at me as if he couldn't understand how this could happen to him. I hit him again, this time across the collarbone. He let out a short yell and fell over backwards. I let him lay there and went toward the dayroom for his partner or partners. There was only one, and he was standing in the doorway, alerted by his friend's yell.

"What's happening, where's brother Jones?" he asked, apparently not seeing the pipe in my hand.

"Brother Jones isn't comin' tonight," I answered,

and swung the pipe into his face. He wailed in pain, then started yelling for help and got it. The lights went on and four guards raced into the dormitory. My two victims had to go to the hospital, but not before the last one I hit told The Man that I'd attacked them first for no apparent reason. I gave my side of the story, but I was still thrown in the maximum detention unit, "the Hole." I guess they figured the two blacks had gotten punishment enough from my beating, because I was the only one who got sent there. My crash course in prison survival had begun; it was a survival that required developing the emotional, mental, and physical sensitivity of an armored combat tank.

The Hole is located in the basement of Cellblock 3, the lockup unit for troublemakers, just behind Death Row. I always thought that was ironic, the two experiences seeming so similar. Like waiting on Death Row for that long, legally delayed date with cyanide, being in the Hole could make a man wish he were dead. There are ten "holes," six-by-nine-foot cells with no windows, no ventilation, no lights; just darkness. Two of them are padded for the more violent resister. Most of the time you're stripped and thrown in naked, as I was. All you're allowed is a thin blanket, a toothbrush, and a metal cup; a mattress is given to you at ten at night and taken away at six in the morning. They feed you one meal every three days, and six slices of white bread for the two days in between. There's a faucet in the cell, but there's water in it only when the guard comes and turns it on from the outside. He does that three times a day, morning, noon, and evening. You've got nothing to store the water in, so you've got to drink what you can, wash up, and fill your cup so you've got some to last till the next time it's turned on.

It's a thirsty stretch from 6:00 P.M. to 6:00 A.M. with one cup of water. The toilet is a hole in the floor that you squat over. It flushes from the outside. The guards think it's funny not to flush it for a few days in a row, playing their little mind games with you. "Does it smell pretty good in there?" they'll ask every time they come by. When it's hot, like it was when I went in that first time, it got to stinking pretty bad. There isn't any toilet paper, either, so even if they kept the thing flushed, after a few days you get to smelling pretty rank yourself. In the winter, it's freezing cold, so you don't have to worry about the odor. You have enough to do trying to keep warm with one thin blanket and no heat. The only time I saw light was when The Man opened the door to give me the mattress or meals. Though I couldn't communicate via visits or letters with anyone from the outside world, I could carry on a yelling conversation with the even more unfortunate dudes on Death Row or with others who'd been thrown in the Hole, or at least I could when someone wasn't screaming to get out or throwing a fit. After three days, I didn't have the energy to carry on much small talk. My thoughts began to give way to fantasies about food, all kinds of food; I'd turn those slices of white bread into pound cake and eat them slowly, chewing each bite until it was liquid, savoring the delicious meal I was making of it in my mind.

At last my ten days were up and I saw light again, at first painful for my unaccustomed eyes. But I wasn't released back into population. The rule was that after a stint in the Hole a convict was sent upstairs to Segregation, Cellblock 3. Compared to my recent dungeon life, Cellblock 3 seemed like the Waldorf, but only for the first day. There was plenty of light now, but I still wasn't allowed any reading material or those little luxury items from the canteen that make prison life bearable, like cigarettes, candy bars, and Kool-Aid. I was still locked up all day and all night in a six-by-nine cell, with clothing and a bed this time, as well as a toilet that I could flush; but there was no exercise, no fresh air. There was more food, but it was hardly edible; it was served on paper plates and 99 percent of the time it was cold because of the long trek from the kitchen to the cellblock. The major diversions were shower time, when three times a week we got to walk the catwalk to the shower, stand under the running water for five minutes, and walk back to our cells; and the weekly one-hour session called exercise time, when we'd be let out of our cells one at a time to walk up and down the corridor and shoot the breeze with the inmates on the same tier. Radios weren't allowed, and there was no TV. Usually three or four days out of seven some con would entertain us all by stuffing a towel in his toilet and flooding the hallway with three or four inches of water. Since we weren't allowed out of our cells, the guards would have to clean it up while we got laughs out of watching them take off their shoes, roll up their pants, and mop away, cussing all the time. Besides that, the only recreation available was writing endless numbers of letters or beating off three times a day to an imaginary lover. Sometimes the noise level would prevent either of these diversions; inmates would start yelling at each other or the guards, beating on the bars for something to do. Idle time is rampant throughout the prison population, but in lockup and the Hole there's nothing *but* idle time. And the mind games the guards pull: holding back the mail and taunting the convict with the fact; denying visiting privileges when the visitor is waiting downstairs after traveling fifty miles to spend her monthly hour talking to her son or lover or husband or brother. Every day in lockup an inmate got fed a little more to hate.

After two weeks in Cellblock 3, the captain called me down to his office and told me he was going to put me back into population. If I hurt anyone else, he told me, I'd be locked up again. I was released from Segregation that day and assigned to another dormitory, right below the first one I'd been in. The word had traveled. When I walked in, two black guys came up to me.

"Listen, man, we heard what happened upstairs. Don't worry about that happenin' here, we don't want no shit to come down," they assured me.

I was given a lot of respect from that day on. I learned how to survive and got thick-skinned and tougher than I'd ever been in the days when I was committing the robberies that put me there. That's why I ended up spending nine years in the joint before I got paroled. I became a member of the white clique, which at that time hadn't turned into anything as serious as the Aryan Brotherhood. It was just a matter of power in numbers, and since there were so few of us in the pen, we let solidarity be our strength. I had plenty of bad examples to follow; bad in terms of the prissy image most of society has for the way a convict *should* learn to behave, but good for hardening me to the rude facts of prison existence.

The administration itself fostered the hardcore education of inmates by throwing newcomers with only one-to-five-year sentences in with someone who had a lot of time, fifty, a hundred years, maybe life. The lifer isn't any too pleased to be looking at a guy better off than he is who's getting out in maybe six months, so there's tension between them. With so much idle time on their hands, that tension builds in their minds and soon they're at each other's throats. All of a sudden this newcomer, who may have come in just wanting to do his time peacefully and get out, is staring at another six months tagged onto his sentence because the older con riled him and The Man labeled him a trouble-maker. The administration, after all, has to be in there with the lifer a lot longer than with the guy who's only doing one to five, so the lifer gets the edge. The Man may play sadistic games with the convicts, but he's also got his sly way of giving in to the power they wield; he doesn't want any outbreaks of rebellion that might catch the public's attention. This is another ex-ample to add to the long list of how little the prison officials care about *rehabilitating* the inmates. When I came in, there were honor units for the dudes who'd been there a long time and were doing their stint peacefully. The administrators could have encouraged these old-timers to get together with the new arrivals and wise them up to what they were up against in population: for instance, how borrowing money or get-ting into any kind of debt could lead to their being beaten, stabbed, or becoming someone's "kid"—a jailhouse punk who runs errands, cleans house, gets butt-fucked, or gives a blow job whenever his "owner" wants; how hardcore cons put pressure on the families of the dudes who owe them money, writing to a friend on the streets that so-and-so owes them, which sends the friend to the guy's wife or relatives, saying, "You gotta pay up on his debt or we're gonna beat his ass in the joint." These peaceful old-timers could have of-fered help to the newcomers in case any of these things came to pass, but they didn't, and the administration didn't ask them to, either. Nothing but survival of the strongest was encouraged in the penitentiary.

It took six years for my hardcore training to throw me into a role I never expected to be in—that of a killer. I was head cook in the kitchen then. One Friday morning a fish (a new inmate) came in from Quarantine to work on the cleanup detail. He was a young, tall, muscular man fresh out of Viet Nam who insisted on being called Eagle Beak and on throwing his weight around to prove what a badass dude he was. He zeroed in on one of my regular Chicano helpers, hassling him all morning with racial innuendos that quickly turned into blatant obscenities and name-calling. My sidekick was handling his end of the abuses just fine, so I didn't step in, figuring the fish would talk himself out. But he got physical about it, walking over and pushing the Chicano against the wall.

"Hey, leave the kid alone," I yelled over to him.

Eagle Beak let go like he was holding a hot coal and came up to me. "Okay, I'll let him alone," he said, then smacked me hard in the jaw with his fist.

Common sense won over my instant reflex to kick the shit out of him. Aside from the fact that he was too large for me to successfully fight with my bare hands, I didn't want to get into it with him right there in the kitchen. I'd worked my way up into a good job—not easy to come by in prison—and I didn't want to blow it over some fish trying to prove he had balls. "Man, that hurt. I wish you wouldn't do that any more," I told him with ominous warning in my voice. He got the message and didn't cause any more trouble for the rest of the day.

The next morning was another matter, though. I was

chopping lettuce for the Sunday salad when Eagle Beak walked up threateningly close and said calmly: "I was thinkin' about what happened yesterday. I figure that the job I did on you wasn't good enough. Let's me and you get down and get it right this time."

I kept on chopping. "Man, I don't want to fight you."

But he popped me again, this time with such force he made my nose bleed. He laughed when he saw the blood and started coming at me again, but the carving knife I was holding reached his belly first. It was a long, French chef's knife that I'd just sharpened that morning, and it pierced him clear through. He groaned and clutched his stomach, and after a few moments of staggering, crumpled to the floor. Someone had to go get the guard; he hadn't been around to hear the fight. Eagle Beak was taken to the hospital, and I was sent to lockup while the administration investigated the event.

Eagle Beak died ten days later. After two weeks in Segregation I was called into the warden's office. To my amazement he told me they weren't going to press murder charges against me. Why? Because the district attorney didn't have a murder weapon. It seems the knife with which I'd killed Eagle Beak was the sharpest one in the kitchen, so the unthinking prison employee who was chief steward cleaned it off and went right on using it. When the D. A. came to the penitentiary to gather his evidence against me, he went to the kitchen and just about blew a fuse when he saw the steward using it to cut a roast. Without the knife, there wasn't a case. I'd gotten tight enough with my co-workers that they didn't go for The Man's promises of reward if they'd come up with a story that would earn a conviction. They just told the truth: It was self-defense, started by the victim. The warden closed our interview by saying, "Well, the guy is dead, he had no friends here, and I know he was pickin' on you. Do you think you can go back to the population and behave yourself?"

Naturally I answered yes.

I didn't get convicted for the killing, but I did pay the prison price. It was on my record and made the parole board deny my release for three more years. At that point I didn't care. I was young and carried an I-don't-give-a-fuck attitude about everything except my own safety and sanity, and that was well-protected. I belonged to a strong clique, and after my bout with Eagle Beak everyone, including myself, thought I was a hot-shit, badass, hardcore, motherfucker that nobody better mess with. The administration thought so, too, and instead of sending me back to a dormitory or cellhouse in regular population, they sent me to the maximum security Cellblock 5, the toughest unit in the penitentiary, where I was surrounded with cons far worse than me.

Here I got a post-graduate education in how to be the baddest bully in the joint, taught by the most incorrigible troublemakers in the prison, some of whom were criminally insane, at least in my book. These men got their rocks off harassing other inmates and watching them snivel in fear. They never fought among each other, but bulldogged the rest of the prison. In fact, they ran the place; even the administration was afraid of them. The top echelon of the Chicano and white cliques lived in Southside 5. A black in the cellblock was unheard of; he wouldn't have lasted an hour. Even a white or Chicano couldn't move in without being "co-signed" by at least two other convicts who lived there; that is, if he valued his life. No one ever tried to bust the party voluntarily, but if they had they'd be faced with thirty men, every one of them wielding a weapon of some sort, whether a pipe, straight razor, shop-made knife, or Molotov cocktail. They had plenty of time on their hands to think about ways of getting and stashing their arsenals and devised some cunning hiding places and smuggling schemes. The administration and the guards knew all of this was happening and would regularly shake down the dorms and cellblocks. (It wasn't just the hardcore cellblock inmates who stashed weapons, though they were the best-armed men in the prison.) But for every knife discovered, there were two to take its place. The convicts took their holding of weapons seriously; it was the only power they had, and often they had saved a dude's ass or life in a fight, as the pipe had for me when I first arrived in the prison. The Man looks the other way for the most part as long as these arsenals are being used by inmates against other inmates. It's only when rumors of a riot came down that the administration makes a real effort to find them.

Most of the cons in Cellblock 5 stayed high on some kind of drug seven days a week. Drugs in the joint were no problem at all, especially for these guys, who could bulldog their way into anything. If you had cash, there was always some underpaid guard eager to make a fast buck and ready to supply you with whatever you needed. And there was a lot of green money floating around the penitentiary, smuggled in during visits, through the legal mail, or via an inmate coming in from the honor unit. Lots of new arrivals who were wise would "kista-stash" (hide in their ass) their cash. They got away with it because in New Mexico there weren't any probing body checks, perhaps because the Catholic unbringing of the mostly Chicano administration and their macho ethic made such precautions repugnant. A bag of grass costing $25 on the street went for $150. You could likewise buy heroin or acid; cocaine was rarer to come by. Commercial booze was also available from guards, but if you weren't flush there was always home-brew, the staple intoxicant of every prison. Cellblock 5 always had a steady supply coming in. It could be made anywhere but in the kitchen most naturally, since that's where all the ingredients were; but the fixings could be smuggled up to the dormitories or cellblocks and put together there. When I worked in the kitchen we'd take a gallon of either raw potatoes, tomato puree, raisins, or anything else that was available and let it ferment, putting it in something large like a five-gallon milk can, filling it two-thirds with water, then adding the gallon of fermenting material plus ten pounds of sugar, and stirring. Then we'd get raw rising dough or yeast from the bakery, mix that in to get the brew cooking, cover it, and put it in a warm place for three or four days until it was ready. It tasted about as good as the ingredients sound, but in the joint it seemed as fine as champagne.

The inmates in Cellblock 5 were left alone to work over whomever they wanted as long as they didn't get in The Man's way. In fact, the administration used Cellblock 5 to do a lot of their dirty work for them. One "house" in the cellblock was always left free so that a new arrival, a fish who'd been giving the guards a hard time, could be thrown in there for a day, sometimes two, to scare him. And it would scare the poor bastard all right. The kid would catch hell, getting beaten, kicked, raped, talked at, and robbed. He'd come out of that cell in a state of shock, wondering what he did to deserve being thrown in with a bunch of maniacs like these. I've seen them dribbling at the mouth with eyes rolled up in their heads when The Man finally came and took them away. I remember one kid who'd just been transferred from Arizona. He thought he was a big shot, so the guards threw him in the empty cell. As soon as The Man left, someone got out his pipe and started in on the kid, hitting him with it all the way down the catwalk to the cellblock doorway. He was taken out then and there and spent some time in the infirmary. The beating struck such fear in him that he asked to do the rest of his time locked up in the protection unit, which he did. Anyone who asked for lockup in protection got it, but he'd have to sign a waiver releasing the penitentiary from any responsibility for what happened to him if he ever wanted to go back into population. He didn't pick an easy solution. Protection is also a twenty-four hour lockup, no exercise, cold-foot stint; and it shot a man't reputation to hell. Anyone who chose not to stand up and fight but to hide instead in the protection unit with the snitches and baby rapers was despised. He was weak—the one thing survivors never allowed themselves to be.

Besides taking care of the administration's troublemakers, the men of Cellblock 5 specialized in personal paybacks. Anyone who burned one of them or their friends was in for disaster: In the joint, where there's little else to think about, old grudges grow to vendetta proportions. One day, a Southside 5 resident I'll call Barnes got word that an old buddy who'd burned him on the streets for $300 worth of dope had just come out of Quarantine and into population. Barnes got two friends to lure the dude up to the cellblock, where only someone new in the joint would dare to go. As they were bringing him up, inmates in Quarantine, which at that time was in Cellblock 4 just across the hall from 5, started warning him not to go in there, but it was too late. Barnes and ten of his close bros were standing in the middle of the catwalk waiting. The welcher was pushed toward them, then dragged into a cell where the eleven men did a job on him. He kept yelling for help, but it didn't do him any good. Only one guard was on duty, and he stood at the door to ask what was going on. He knew very well what was happening, but he was too chickenshit to come in. Instead he made a beeline to the office phone to call for assistance. He was stopped by four Chicanos who'd been stationed to watch for just such possibilities. They got to him just as he was about to dial, and surrounding but not touching him, warned: "Man, you better get the fuck off the phone and disappear for a while or we're gonna get you on the floor, too."

The officer knew they meant it and split. He couldn't have done anything for the welcher anyway. By then the poor guy was nearly beaten to death. His teeth were knocked out, both eyes were blackened, and his nose was broken and bloody. When they were finished working him over, they dragged his unconscious body across the hall and dumped it in Cellblock 4, Quarantine. All thirty residents of Cellblock 5 followed, walking into the unit as if we lived there. It was payback time for their getting involved in warning the welcher. A few noses were busted and eyes blackened, then Barnes stopped the action and asked: "Okay, any of you friends of this guy, any of you want to speak up for him?" There was silence. There were thirty of us and seventy of them, but we'd completely subdued them. Barnes decided that while he was there he might as well take a little treasure. Shaking a pillow out of its case, he announced, "Okay, every one of you sons of bitches, throw your canteen into this sack." Each of us grabbed ourselves a pillowcase and got into the act, walking up and down the catwalk in partners, going into each cell and strongarming everyone in Quarantine for their precious stashes and valuables; everyone except four or five old-timers back on repeats. But the newcomers were told, "Come on, load it up, *all* your smokes, son, and give me that watch off your arm, and that ring." We left with at least fifteen sacks full of food, cigarettes, and jewelry. Not until we were back in Cellblock 5 did a guard show up on the scene asking if everything had cooled down. He was told that everything was cool but that there was a pretty sick fish passed out in Quarantine. When he left to check it out, we could hear the guys in 4 yelling to him. "They robbed us, those motherfuckers, they creamed us." The screw told them he thought they were exaggerating, and they'd be better off forgetting the whole thing.

So Cellblock 5 was victorious again. Instead of getting thrown in the Hole for our violence, that night we partied with $500 worth of smokes, candy, Kool-Aid, potato and taco chips, cocoa, and the instant coffee we'd pillaged, making deals for the rings and watches that were part of the booty. From then on, the fishes in Quarantine had trouble keeping their canteen. They'd go to the store, get their weekly supply of goodies, and get zapped when they came down the main corridor toward the unit. It didn't matter how big or small he was, the average fish got ripped off. Only if he was an old-timer was he let go. Sometimes they'd put up a fight, but it would be madness to try and fight off ten dudes. The guards continued to look the other way. I guess they figured that if those hardass cons in 5 were keeping themselves happy taking away canteens, then they wouldn't be hassling them. In the fourteen years I was at the pen, there were many turnovers in Cellblock 5 residents, but they always carried on in the same bulldog manner.

When I came back on a new conviction after being paroled in 1974, it took me twelve of those fourteen years to take a look at my life and decide it was time I grew up; the prison had gotten even worse. It was so overcrowded that there weren't enough jobs or programs to keep the inmates occupied, so idleness was their major activity; this meant hundreds of men sitting around the dayrooms and dormitories all day long with nothing to do but shoot the shit and scheme on how to get one over on The Man or how to work over some personal or racial enemy. Besides the idle time, the sardine living conditions were giving the cons a lot to be angry about.

Researchers at the Yale School of Medicine recently did a study that proved scientifically, in case no one had noticed the real-life proof, the dangerous effects of overcrowded dormitories in prison. They found that inmates living in this situation experienced an increase in blood pressure; that overcrowding caused stress and tension and required a "high degree of vigilance by inmates,"[2] which involved a loss of personal control and disrupted social relationships. The most natural way to express the frustration was to find a scapegoat. Prison, it's often said, is a reflection of society, and society isn't finished with its racial prejudices; they'd rubbed off on every convict when he was on the streets and growing up, and he carried them into the jungle with him, where the pressure made his bigotry a mountain of resentment. Seldom were there out-and-out race wars with ten or twenty members of each clique fighting each other; more often clique grudges were carried out in one-to-one stabbings. The majority of the "wars," though, were waged by attitude and talk. And organization.

The rising crime rate had brought more whites and blacks into the penitentiary. By 1980, 53 percent of the population was Chicano/Hispanic; 37 percent Anglo, 9 percent black, and 1 percent Indian. The edge was not just in number for the Chicano. Most of the prison personnel were of Mexican-Spanish origin. In the early days, when 75 percent of the inmates were Chicano, The Man looked on them as ordinary convict scum and treated them like the same pieces of dirt as the other convicts. Now that they had scapegoats not only for their pretensions of self-righteousness but for their racial prejudices as well, they began to show favoritism toward their Chicano brothers. This didn't make the Anglos, once allies, feel any too safe with the Mexican clique. Though there had been a white clique all along, it wasn't until 1973, when bikers from the west coast began to get busted in New Mexico for running drugs cross-country, that the hardcore Aryan Brotherhood began to get a grip on the whites. The bikers reacted strongly to being the underdog to, as they would say, "an inferior race of Mexicans"; they also got a lot of heat from everyone in the joint— Chicanos, blacks, the administration, even some whites—because everyone was leery of the ominous and infamous legend of bikers. They decided to form their own group, a prison motorcycle club without the choppers, to be sure their backs were covered in case any of their numerous enemies decided to be brave. The head honcho of this biker clique was the ex-resident of a southwest club, a lifer in for murdering another biker in a shootout between rival gangs. As the California cyclists began to come into the prison in greater numbers, they started touting the Aryan Brotherhood. "Why just form a clique for bikers?" they argued. "There's power in numbers. Let's get the A.B. in and all the white bros in the joint can join." They wrote to the California headquarters of the American Nazi Party for the right to open a chapter in the Penitentiary of New Mexico, got permission, and soon just about every white con in the place was a full-fledged member. For the first time in the prison's history the whites had a clique to equal the long-standing Mexican Mafia of the Chicanos. The blacks, the brunt of both cliques' hatred, were aligned with the Black Muslims. The Black Panthers never gained a foothold in New Mexico like they had in other prisons because in Santa Fe blacks were in the minority.

Most of the convicts who belonged to the cliques were not only uneducated, they looked down on anyone who tried to better themselves. They aimed to make everyone believe they were cold, bad mother-fuckers, and their attitude was, "What bad motherfucker would go to school?" Their main theme was excuses for being in the joint. The blacks thought they were there because of their color; the Chicanos because they were being persecuted by the Anglos, who'd been oppressing Hispanics since they invaded their land a hundred years ago; and the whites said they were there because they didn't have the bucks for high-powered attornies. These were men who were unwilling to face up to their own responsibility for their situations. They'd all talk about the unfairness of society and The Man, but they'd never admit to playing the same game when they infringed on a new convict's freedom by hassling him for protection money or a piece of ass. Let a guard put them in the Hole for some of their carryings on, though, and they'd be the first to snivel that they were being treated unfairly.

I criticize them like an ex-alcoholic criticizes a drunkard because watching them was like watching a part of myself I wanted to forget. I'm not excusing society for its part in shaping a criminal or denying that the prison administration destroys a man's morale and often his mind. But I'm not letting the clique heavies off the hook either, because they do just as much to stop growth and keep anger festering. It's from their ranks that the cruelest rioters came, the ones who would commit atrocities no animal but the human would think of.

V

The last time I went to see him, my brother asked him, when will you be getting out of here? And he said, I think the time I get out of here will be in a coffin.

—MOTHER OF JOE MADRID[1],
Inmate #25940
Penitentiary of New Mexico

2:15 A.M., Saturday, February 2, 1980. "What's goin' on?" a captain of the Black Muslims asked guardedly as a Chicano rioter unlocked his cell.

Three white militants moved in front of the open door before the black could get out. "Brother, this is a riot. You got five minutes to talk to your people and find out if they're with us or not."

The Muslim nodded mutely and the men turned and left the cellhouse. The black walked out onto the catwalk and saw that only the few Chicanos and whites housed in the predominately black Cellhouse 6 had been released by the rioters.

"All right, brothers, as you can see, this is a riot, and

61

whitey and the Mex want to know if we're with them or against them in this shit." He started cranking open cells while he spoke. "Some of you gotta go spread the word to the other brothers on the south side; tell them we're gonna meet in here, in five, man—these dudes are anxious." There was no ceiling separating the first and second tiers of the cellhouse, so everyone in the unit could hear his booming voice. Some of the blacks went out into the prison to get their brothers, others went up to the second tier and started unlocking those cell doors. Soon the second tier dayroom and catwalk were filled with every black in the prison except those locked up in Protection. The Muslim captain stood in the middle of the noisy crowd of men, raising voice and hands to quiet them.

"Listen, brothers—you see what's comin' down. Now, what do we do, stay out or get into it? I think if we don't get in it we'll have to get down with every whitey and Mex in this joint. I'm for raising hell with The Man. . . ."

The crowd shouted their approval, but the speaker interrupted them. "But," his booming voice got their attention, "we've got to make this unit and the old men's dormitory our territorial line. If we spread too thin, whitey might want to fuck with some of our brothers. And one more thing: Our minister is in Protection. We have to make getting him out of there our first priority. Once they get in, there's gonna be deep trouble, and we don't want him messed with. . . ."

He stopped because movement at the door caught his eye. Ten Aryan Brothers and twice as many of the Mexican Mafia were coming into the vestibule at the front of the unit, some of them standing on the stairs, blocking the exit. They looked as if they were ready to go to war then and there if they got the wrong answer. "Well, what's it going to be?"

"Count us in; my people are as tired of The Man fucking us over as you are. It's payback time all right. There's just one deal we have to make."

"What's that?"

"We want to get Jeff Brewster out of Protection when you get in there—and I mean, we want to be the first to enter and get him the fuck out before anything comes down."

The militant group spokesmen in the front lines looked at each other for silent advice and nodded approval.

"Okay with us."

"Well, we're with you then; you need us, you'll always find someone right here, cause this is gonna be our headquarters."

"All right. We brought you some goodies to celebrate, here." Shoeboxes of pills and syringes were passed through the crowd to toast the pact. For this night at least, there was peace among the races; peace for the sake of a greater war.

The rioters who'd gone back to the control center to look for the keys to Cellblock 3 were having trouble finding them in the debris. In their impatience to get their friends out of lockup, the group waiting at the cellblock door decided to go down to the basement where they'd seen Officer Mendoza run after he'd refused to open the upstairs grill.

They demanded now that he unlock this gate, which led to the maximum detention units, the bottom tier of Cellblock 3. But again Officer Mendoza refused.

"Let's go get us a hostage to make him change his mind, what say, bro?" The bros said agreed and off they went to Dormitory E-2. They returned dragging Captain Roybal and slammed his face up against the bars of the locked grill.

"Okay, Mendoza, if you're brave enough to take a look from your hiding place, you'll see we've got your old Captain Roybal here. He ain't very comfortable; he's been beaten pretty bad. This shank we're holding to his throat's only gonna make him feel worse, 'cause if you don't open the door, Mendoza, we're gonna slit his head off his shoulders and roll it down the aisle."

The officer didn't have to make a decision.

"Hey, man, fuck those pigs, we found the keys," a Chicano rioter said, running up to the group. "They were buried under a ton of shit down there. Someone must've knocked 'em down when we tore it apart."

They fumbled with the keys and had difficulty finding the right one. In the interim, the three guards came out of their hiding closet and locked themselves behind another grill. When they finally succeeded in unlocking the gate and were inside, the officers surrendered. They were roughed up, hit across the legs with pipes, spit on, cursed at, but their treatment was nowhere near as brutal as that of the first seven guards captured. They were ordered to strip naked, then shoved into a cell and locked in for the duration of the riot.

"Hey, what's goin' on out there?" a voice called from one of the maximum detention units. They have solid steel doors with no windows, so the man could only hear that a ruckus was going on. Perhaps he didn't believe his ears when it sounded like his fellow convicts were in control.

"It's a riot, man. We've taken over the joint. Who're you?"

"Primi Martinez—far out, let me outta this fuckin' hole so I can join you, will ya?"

"*Ohhhh*—good old Archie Martinez, eh?"

"Primi baby, is that really you all locked up in that dungeon? Primi Martinez, the king of the snitches? Nah, man, we're not gonna let you out; we're gonna come in there and show you how much we appreciate all you've done for us, Primi—y'know what we mean, so you can really feel it, right down to your prick."

There was silence from the cell. Primi Martinez was busy jamming his toothbrush in the crack of his door so it couldn't be cranked open. Just in time, too. The rioters were in front of his cell as he got it in place. When the crank wouldn't move, they demanded he open the door.

"Fuck you, no way," he answered, his tone more surly than afraid.

"If you don't, we're gonna do you real bad when we do get in there. And we'll get in, Primi, so make your confession, bro, cause your day has come."

Most of this was said in their native language. Homeboy or no, Archie Martinez was the biggest snitch in the joint. There were a lot of men in Cellblock 3 who he'd put there and a lot of rioters he'd informed on. They vowed they'd be back with some of the men he'd snitched on and better weapons to deal with him; specifically they had in mind a blowtorch they knew was kept in the basement plumbing shop.

The group moved along the hallway, asking who was inside each of the units as they went. They unlocked three or four inmates who were from population. But when they heard the name Juan Sanchez, someone remembered that he was "that crazy sonofabitch" that a buddy of theirs had had a beef with.

Juan Sanchez was a Mexican national who'd been placed in the protection unit because he was genuinely insane, not because he was a snitch; but even those in Protection can get thrown in the Hole if they get wild, and Juan Sanchez often got wild. That he hadn't been sent to the forensic unit in Las Vegas, New Mexico, instead of the joint always amazed everyone. From the moment Sanchez had come into the prison, his behavior smacked of derangement. He'd tried to kill himself several times, cutting his arms open with a razor the first time. Then he turned his attacks on other inmates. He would get delusional and talk about seeing visions of the devil and Jesus Christ. All this earned him the label of paranoid schizophrenic from the psychological department plus lockup, first in Cellblock 3, then in the protection unit. It also brought the wrath of the guards, who would beat him up constantly for no good reason except that they were tired of his babbling. In March of 1979, he complained to them that his sink was stopped up. Their response was to call the goon squad, who did their usual lesson-teaching routine, hitting him in the back, ribs, and head with their clubs before throwing him into the Hole. Naked, of course. Juan Sanchez might have been crazy, but he had enough marbles to write a letter to the Mexican Consulate shortly thereafter, in May of 1979, asking to be transferred to Mexico as part of the U.S.–Mexico prisoner transfer treaty happening at the time. "The officials of the institution and the prisoners are torturing me," his letter began. A fight with another prisoner, he said, had caused an inmate to threaten to kill him. "How are you going to kill me when we are locked in separate cells in Cellblock 3?" he had asked the inmate. "He said he was going to take my life and has played cards and never lost a game." The inmate began harassing him, calling him a *gallina* ("coward") and *ioto* ("homosexual"). In fact, he wrote the Consulate, both prisoners and prison officials taunted him about his courage and his manhood. "I heard on the official loudspeaker that I had confessed to the gringos and Chicanos that I was a coward and a homosexual. . . . They were playing with my honor as a man, torturing me mentally, withholding food, trying to humiliate me."[2]

But the Mexican Consulate didn't take immediate enough action to save Juan Sanchez. A rioter armed with a tear gas gun opened his cell door and walked in. Juan Sanchez was standing in a corner mumbling to himself. The light let in by the open door blinded him, unaccustomed as he was to anything but days of darkness in the Hole; so he didn't see the man come up to him and fire the tear gas canister into his face. Maybe he didn't even feel his head explode. Maybe Juan Sanchez died peacefully with the help of his delusional angels.

His murderer and this small band of rioters now turned their attention to the original business: freeing their buddies upstairs in Cellblock 3. They dragged the naked and badly battered Captain Roybal along with them instead of returning him to Dormitory E-2. This was a smart move on their part. They had the key to the unit's main grill, but the gates at the entrance of each row of cells were controlled by a panel they didn't know how to operate. A shank was held to Captain Roybal's throat once again as he was forced to show them how the panel worked. When the first tier was opened, four or five of the men ran down the corridors shouting the good news and cranking open

cells. The inmates in the cellblock began whooping
and cheering and yelling to be let out. "Hurry up,
brother, let's get this goddamned grill open so I can get
out of here. We've got work to do. It's about time we
fucked up this place. . . . " Their uproar could be heard
all over the north side of the prison. Many of these
men had been locked up for six months or more; the
prospect of getting out of their cells and having the
freedom to move—not to mention the added incentive
of revenge—wound them up with excitment. While the
inmates on the second tier were being released, the
rest of this band of rioters dragged Roybal up to the
third tier and forced him to show them how to operate
that control panel. Then they locked him in the first
cell opened, where he stayed for the duration of the
riot, naked, no doubt cold and wondering if he'd ever
come out of this alive, listening to the convicts going
wild as more and more of them were set free.

A lieutenant of the Aryan Brotherhood, one of the
original riot instigators from Dormitory E-2, ran up
and down the aisles looking for two of his close buddies, also bikers and honchos in the brotherhood.
They'd been locked up since they'd been captured
after escaping in the December breakout of eleven inmates. When he found one, the first words out of his
friend's mouth were, "Well, brother, looks like you
guys got your shit together. Hurry up and get the door
open so I can get the hell out of this sonofabitch." The
lieutenant obliged, and the two of them went down the
corridor until they came to the third member of this
triumverate and cranked his door open; these three
stayed close while they helped their other bros unlock
all the whites in Segregation. Meanwhile, the Chicanos
were busy unlocking their clique, and the blacks

theirs, until all eighty-six inmates in lockup—men the administration labeled as the most dangerous in the prison—were free. Most of the fourteen-member execution squad—a squad that would soon deal death to those they judged guilty of crimes against the convict ethic—came from among these inmates. Chicanos, whites, and blacks were represented on this execution squad.

When all the Aryan Brotherhood had been freed, they gathered in the middle tier of the cellblock.

"The first thing we have to do is get ourselves some weapons," one of the leaders said. "And the best place to get them is in the kitchen. . . . "

"The next thing we gotta get is the snitches," another interrupted, gathering noisy agreement from his colleagues.

"Right on, so let's fuckin' *go!*"

The group stormed down the corridor to the kitchen, broke into the steward's office, where they knew the knives were locked in a cabinet at night, and in ten minutes had the cabinet open and themselves armed with butcher knives and meat cleavers. These weapons didn't go unused for long. On the way out of the kitchen, the biker triumverate bumped into a one-armed old-timer who wasn't well-liked because he'd once refused to join the Aryan Brotherhood. When the three saw him, they decided to give him his payback. Pulling their knives out, they pointed them at his throat and belly and told him to get up against the wall. He did as he was told, but his obedience didn't save him. He was slammed on the head with a riot stick and knocked to the floor.

"Hold him down, man, I've always wanted to fuck a man with no arms." The biker's two companions did as he asked while he pulled a long carving knife out of his belt and started sawing through the skin and muscles of the man's only arm. The old-timer wasn't any slouch. Whether through fear or pain, he managed to wriggle and wrestle his way free of the two rioters holding him down, kneeing his attacker off of him and running for his life down the smokey, crowded corridor. The three didn't bother chasing him, they just laughed. "Fuck him," one said, "we'll get back to him later. We've got more important shit to take care of." The one-armed old-timer didn't lose life or limb; but the tendons and muscles were cut so severely that the use of his only arm is now seriously impaired, a hard way to go in the world, but triply hard in prison.

Bands of rioters in search of weapons and destruction had followed the whites into the kitchen and were breaking into the storerooms, taking everything that could be used for violence, from rolling pins to cast-iron pans, as well as food to stash in the dorms and cellhouses. They tore the place apart, breaking windows and all the glassware, smashing tables and chairs, pulling out electrical wiring, ripping out the plumbing and flooding the floor. They destroyed everything they could. Other gangs were wrecking the canteen, taking all the candy, coffee, and clothing they were able to carry, stocking up for the hours, possibly days, they thought the riot might last. Still others were downstairs in the basement raiding the shops for new additions to their arsenal. In the plumbing shop they found the *crème de la crème* of weapons, a heavy-duty acetylene cutting torch. And in the paint and shoe repair shops they discovered the favorite high of many of the convicts, "sniff"—paint, paint thinner, and glue—

available in large quantities. The drugs found in the hospital were mainly downers that should have made the inmates more mellow than violent; but mixed with "sniff," known to induce ferocious behavior, the tranquilizers became energizers.

The group that found the cutting torch dragged it upstairs to the end of the south side corridor where the educational unit and Dormitory D, with eighty-six inmates still in it, were closed off from the rest of the prison by a grill for which the rioters had no key. They turned the torch on the bars of the grill until they cut it open, released the inmates, some of whom were new arrivals housed on the first floor in the admissions and orientation or quarantine units of the dorm, and took Officer Michael Hernandez, who'd hidden himself in the educational section, as hostage. Hernandez was twenty-five years old and had only been at the institution for four months. He was initiated into prisoner violence by feeling their pipes and clubs beating down on him. Fortunately for him, the rioters were anxious to get on with other massacres, so they didn't spend a lot of time assaulting Hernandez.

With the release of Dormitory D, every inmate in the institution was free to roam the prison except the ninety-six men locked up in Cellblock 4, the protection unit.

Down the corridor from Dormitory D, an angry mob had gathered outside the door of E-1, the semi-protection unit whose inmates had barricaded themselves in. Residents of E-1 were younger men who had problems being in general population, problems like getting raped and harassed for money. They needed protection not because they were snitches but because they were not able to grow the teeth it takes to survive in the convict jungle. They didn't need to be caged in lone cells twenty-four hours a day because they were neither troublemakers nor informers, but whenever they ventured out into the main corridor they were escorted by guards, and though they ate in the mess hall, it was at a different time than the rest of the population. These were men who just wanted to serve their time and get out without being touched by the bizarreness they'd experienced in the mainstream of prison life. In the eyes of most convicts, however, they were simply weak. Many of these inmates had enemies among the population, and all of them knew that by choosing their protected status, they were despised. They were therefore naturally leery of the coaxing words being spoken by the rioters outside their door.

"Hey now, why don't you guys take that shit down and come on out and join us. As far as being mad at you, we're not. Let bygones be bygones; we're all together now, and all we want to do is fight The Man."

Their refusal infuriated the mob.

"You sons-of-bitches either come out now or we're gonna come in and drag you out, and if we have to do that we're gonna fuck up a whole bunch of you real bad."

"Fuck you," someone from inside the dorm yelled out. "We're not leaving. You want us, you come on in and get us if you can."

The door was solid on the bottom, but the upper half had twelve six-by-eight-foot wire-meshed windows in it which the rioters began pummelling with pipes and clubs until there were jagged holes in several of them. Someone then aimed a tear-gas gun at one of the openings, hoping the canister would fall into the dormitory and choke out the men inside. Instead, it missed, bouncing off the door into the corridor and exploding among the aggressors. They moved away, coughing and cursing, but when the gas had cleared enough for them to deal with it, they came back, determined now to have their way. By the sheer weight of a group push they attempted to shove the door open but succeeded only in creating a four- or five-inch gap. Beyond that, the barricade of bunk beds, tables, and chairs held. One of the rioters tried crawling through this small opening, but as soon as he stuck his arm in, an E-1 resident slammed a chair leg down on it hard enough to break his wrist.

"Sonofabitch, you broke my arm. I'll kill you, you no good cocksucker."

The rioters conferred. Someone got the bright idea to smoke them out. Dragging blankets, mattresses, newspapers, and pillows in front of the door, they set fire to them, but this time, too, their plan failed. The men in E-1 were ready, and fanned the smoke that seeped in back out into the corridor. Once again their tormenters had to disperse for air.

Among this group of rioters was an inmate named Joe Madrid. He wasn't mad at anyone in E-1; in fact, he had a few friends in the unit. He'd been talking to one of those friends earlier, trying to convince him that it would be better all around for them to come out. Now he understood his friend's reticence. While the rest of the group was off trying to find a place to breathe, Joe called his buddy over to the barricade.

"Listen, I think the best thing for you guys to do is get outside the prison and give yourselves up to The Man."

"Yeah, that's a good idea, Joe, but how? We don't

have anything in here we can get the windows out with."

"A pipe wrench will do it. I'll go find one in one of the shops downstairs. I'll be back."

In a few minutes Joe returned with a three-foot wrench. As he was handing it to his friend through the opening in the barricade, the rioters were returning and saw the transaction.

"Hey, you sonofabitch," one of them called to him. "If they get out because of you, your ass is in trouble."

"Hey, man, some of those guys in there are my friends, and I don't think they should be hassled," Joe tried to explain to this group of mostly fellow Chicanos.

His explanation didn't hold. People began yelling, shouting curses at him; finally someone came from behind and hit him over the head with a riot stick. The blow drew blood and knocked Joe to the ground. The mob began attacking him with their pipes and clubs, kicking and beating him mercilessly; beating the life out of him.

"Hey, man, I think he's dead."

When the rioters realized that indeed their victim had stopped breathing, they dragged his body the length of the corridor to the gymnasium, where others were busy tearing apart that facility. There they got a fifteen-foot length of rope. They would use it to demonstrate the proper treatment for the body of a traitor, for to them, homeboy or no, Joe Madrid was a traitor; he'd gone aginst them in favor of the weaklings. Tying the rope under his arms and around his chest, they strung him up on the basketball hoop for all to see. There he would hang for the rest of the riot: Joe Madrid, serving a one-to-five year sentence for possession of narcotics, dead at thirty-eight because he tried to be a nice guy in the penitentiary of the Land of Enchantment. During those hours of madness that were to follow, inmates would come in and hack at his dangling corpse with knives, beat it with pipes, mutilating it so totally that it was beyond recognition, a raw bloody mass of flesh by the time the uprising was over.

But then, violence is inherent in the Land of Enchantment and in the Chicano culture. It's the land of the Penitente, the self-flagellating Catholics of northern New Mexico who whip themselves in private to scourge the sins of their soul. At Easter they do one of their lot the honor of crucifying him in the enactment of Christ's death on the cross. This Cristo doesn't die, however. No nails are used, but his wrists and feet are tied to a cross, which he carries many long miles to the crucifixion site while his friends whip him as he goes, just as the Christ he's portraying was tormented along the road to Calvary. Those in the procession are equally penitent, lashing themselves with sticks, whips, and sometimes cactus. Los Hermanos Penitentes is one of the few folk religions alive in the world today. It developed when the Spanish priests had to leave the land in 1828 because of their nation's dwindling empire. These class-conscious friars had steadfastly resisted taking into the priesthood the mixed-blood natives—the mestizo blend of Spanish, Mexican and Indian—so when they left there were only a handful of men trained in the rituals of the Church. Since these serviced the more accessible areas, the people of the isolated mountain country were left to their own spiritual devices. They chose to worship what they experienced so much of in the cold, stark mountains of the north: pain and death.

Archie Martinez came from that north country. Chimayo is in the northern mountains of New Mexico, but it's not only Penitente land; in Chimayo resides the "Lourdes of America," El Santuario de Chimayo, with its magic mud. Travelers from around the world flock there year-round to heal their diseases by spreading the moist sand on themselves. Crutches, leg braces, rosaries, dog tags, and drivers licenses all hang on the ancient adobe walls of the Santuario testifying to the mud's miraculous properties. The only miracle it didn't perform was changing poverty to wealth, at least not for Archie Martinez. So he took those matters into his own hands and began robbing his neighbors' houses. He was quite successful at this endeavor. Since there are no police in the village community, it proved to be an easy livelihood. No matter what traps the villagers would set, Archie Martinez always eluded them. He was so swift and slippery that the townsfolk began to build a legend around him: Archie Martinez could only be escaping them because he turned into a "fleet-footed dog"; they began to call him the Dog Boy of Chimayo.[3] But every dog has his day, and Archie wound up at the Penitentiary of New Mexico. Even here he tried his "Dog Boy" routine; in the six years he'd been in prison, he tried twice to escape. These attempts only netted him more time: ten to fifty years for the first try, two to ten for the second. All this, plus his reputation as king of the snitches, the fleet-footed Dog Boy of Chimayo had accomplished in only twenty-five years of living.

Besides being king of the snitches, Archie Martinez was cursed with an obnoxious personality. During his first years in population he'd always been in on the rapes of the new young inmates; he and four or five of his bros would pull a train on the guy, take his canteen, then make him pay protection money. But soon his snitching routine hit the grapevine—here his fleet-footedness failed him—and for the sake of his life's safety he had to spend his time locked up day and night in Protection; or in the Hole. When his big mouth wasn't snitching, it was getting him in trouble with the guards. He was in the Hole this time for cursing and throwing a cup of coffee at one of them.

Now the execution squad, armed with an acetylene cutting torch, came to give Archie his payback for years of informing on them.

"Hey, Arch, we're back. You don't have to open the door, man, we've got a key of our own," they told him.

At first his response was a surly, "The fuck you do." But when he heard the roar of the torch and felt its heat aimed at the steel door, he changed his attitude. "Look, man, I don't want no trouble; why do you want me?"

They told him while they were burning through the door, naming instances when they'd been locked up or thrown in the Hole because he'd told The Man about their activities.

He denied everything. "No, man, it wasn't me, I didn't do that. Why don't you let me out so I can join you?"

"No, Primi, we want your ass. Did you say those prayers, boy, 'cause you better make your peace while you can."

"Listen, I'll take the jam off my door, just let me come out on my own, what do you say?"

"Nah, it's more fun this way. Yeah, Primi, we're gonna have some fun with you, baby. We're gonna turn this torch all over your snivelling body, nice and slow so's you can feel it. Then when you're nice and toasted, we'll cut your dick off and let you taste it."

The door fell off the hinges and they pushed it open. Archie Martinez was standing against the far wall, clutching a mattress to his naked body. They dragged him out of the cell and upstairs to the first tier of Cellblock 3 while he screamed, *"No era yo, no lo hice,"* ("It wasn't me, I didn't do it.") They handcuffed his arms and legs spread-eagle to the bars that lined the wall of the guard station in the front of the cellblock, for they were going to make this a public execution, and began their rite of torture. His screams could be heard not only on the north side but also far into the main corridor that ran through the penitentiary.

They started by beating him with pipes, riot sticks, and chains, breaking his legs, knocking out his teeth, and bloodying his face, doing God-knows-what-kind of internal injury as the clubs hammered his chest and stomach. The beating was so intense that he passed out, but one of the squad went to the hospital and came back with smelling salts, bringing him to consciousness so he could witness the pain of their next torment. Taking a straight razor, they slit the skin over both eyelids and gouged out his eyeballs, so they hung down on his cheeks. Again he passed out and again he was brought around with the smelling salts, this time so he could take one last look at the world through his changed perspective and witness the sudden blackout as they sliced through the optic nerves. The eyeballs fell to the floor, and one of the squad picked them up. "Hey, Arch, I got your eyeballs to remember you by," he taunted, running the bottle of salts under his victim's nose. As he came to, he pleaded with them to kill him and let him die, but they laughed. "No, Arch, we got more in store for you." They brought the razor down on his penis and sliced it off. The smelling salts brought him around just as they were jamming it into his already bloodied mouth. Now they turned the acetyline torch on him, slowly burning each part of his body, first his chest, then his stomach, his face, hands, legs, what was left of his genitals, stopping once to administer the smelling salts and bring him to, rotating the torch among themselves. The Dog Boy of Chimayo would never regain consciousness. The execution squad kept on burning him until they saw he was dead. Then they took his body down and left it lying there for all to see. It was so mutilated that it took hours to find out who it was when the riot was over. But that would be many more horror-filled hours later.

VI

The character and mentality of the keepers may be of more importance in understanding prisons than the character and mentality of the kept. Would that the hordes of researchers who now invade the prisons . . . explore their childhood traumas, flip inkblots to find out what their Rorschach tests reveal, generally try to discover what makes them tick and what made them choose this occupation in the first place. For after all, if we were to ask a small boy, "What do you want to be when you grow up?" and he were to answer, "A prison guard," should we not find that a trifle worrying—cause, perhaps, to take him off to a child guidance clinic for observation and therapy?

—JESSICA MITFORD[1]

Felix Rodriguez, the granddaddy of corrections in New Mexico, began his career as a guard at the Penitentiary, as did many of his friends. "There was a group of officers there who'd grown up together.

These guys came home from the Korean War, and the major industry in Santa Fe was the Department of Corrections. A group of them got in there in 1953, 1954, and stayed there. Felix was the father, the paternal, benevolent dictator of the penitentiary," Tony Anaya, the ex-Attorney General who succeeded in having Rodriguez removed from his position as warden told a reporter after the riot.[2] As is the custom of New Mexico's eternally Democrat-run government and its bag of political party favors, Rodriguez was not thrown out of the Department of Corrections all together; in spite of evidence that he headed an administration heavily involved in drug trafficking and prisoner intimidation, he was given another position in the Department, albeit outside the prison. As testament to his power, at the time of the 1980 riot, five years after he was ousted, Felix Rodriguez was Deputy Secretary of Corrections, the man who ran the whole show. By then he and his cronies were known as the Santa Fe Eleven, the clique that had for twenty years controlled the Penitentiary of New Mexico as if it were their own private empire.[2a]

I'd watched this clique strengthen since I came into the prison in 1962. You might say we all grew tough together. By 1970 the clique had become firmly entrenched in the five top positions inside the penitentiary, and everyone who held an important management post was an active member of it. The only people who kept their jobs were those who played the game the clique's way. The majority of prison personnel, including all the top five members, were Chicano. Nepotism, that familiar abuse of power, kept it that way. Anyone with a plum position was related to or a friend of someone high up in the administration. To

wit, in 1971 Warden Rodriguez's administrative assistant married a personnel technician at the institution.
Not only could they talk to each other about work over
supper, but at family gatherings they could discuss it
with the administrative assistant's brother, who was
the business manager, as well as with the brother's
nephew, the prison storekeeper.[3] If by chance a man
who wasn't well connected got hired, he'd end up with
night shift in the guard tower, the worst job in the
pirson, until he proved he was willing to play according to the clique's rules.

Felix Rodriguez, the leader of the clique, started in
the prison system in 1955 and worked his way up
through the ranks, from guard to lieutenant to associate warden to deputy warden. It was in this last
position that he began to assume the power he'd been
building throughout the years, for in Santa Fe it was
the deputy warden who actually ran the penitentiary.
When Rodriguez became warden in 1970, he secured
the muscle of his clique by promoting tried and trusted
cronies to the four deputy and associate warden positions. In spite of their bitter feelings about this clique,
the convicts respected Rodriguez himself. He was fair,
his word could be trusted, and he was never one to
side only with the guards. If he thought there was
merit to an inmate's complaint, he'd call the officer in,
listen to both stories, and be as likely to reprimand the
guard as he would the inmate. Rodriguez had other
aspects, however, which put him in the same category
as the rest of his henchmen: He had a tendency to
throw temper tantrums and to hold grudges. If he
thought a convict was scheming to deal drugs or stash
weapons, or if he caught him at it, or even if he just
didn't like the con's attitude, he's keep him on his

blacklist forever; no matter how good the inmate's record might become, he wouldn't be able to get a job, a cellblock change, or enroll in an educational program. And Rodriguez always knew who was doing what. The snitch system was his baby, and he kept it running smoothly with promises of privileges and threats of none. As he soft-pedaled the phenomenon to the press, "You have to establish your network so that you're informed about everything that is happening. Most prisoners want to do their time in the easiest way possible and don't want trouble. Some of the intelligence, or information, that comes from prisoners is a result of that desire for quiet."[4] Quiet my butt; the only quiet an informer got was relief from the flack the administration would give him if he didn't snitch.

Rodriguez and his clique were as avid in maintaining their power and their snitch circuits as they were their philosophy that punishment was the way to rehabilitate the criminal mind. Only for ten months in its long history did the Penitentiary of New Mexico have at its helm an inmate-oriented warden, and the shortness of his term speaks for the difficulty he had in establishing his humane policies. Rodriguez had been acting warden for the year it took to find a new man to follow Harold Cox, who'd been in the top position for seven years. When J. E. Baker came into the institution in 1968, Rodriguez went back to being deputy warden; this time, however, he had trouble wielding his usual power. Warden Baker had ideas of his own as well as the strength to impose them on his unwilling staff. The most radical change he made was the abolition of the maximum detention unit as a disciplinary vehicle. Though Rodriguez and his group argued that punishment was an integral part of keeping the inmates under control and the maximum detention unit the most effective method of enforcing that control, Baker stuck to his plan and <u>closed down the Hole</u>. This made a lot of the officers unhappy, but the convicts began to see that not all representatives of law enforcement were pigs. That is not to say they didn't <u>take undue advantage of the new liberality</u> and <u>give the guards a bad time</u>; often they did, for revenge is sweet. They knew nothing serious was going to happen any more if they were written up for an infraction of the rules, that the threats the officers made were hollow, for they had no means of carrying them out. If an inmate felt a guard was treating him unfairly, he knew he could go over his head straight to the warden and find a sympathetic ear. This gave the convicts leeway to bait the guards, to speak their minds more freely. Consequently, during this period there was a large turnover in prison personnel. These guards had not been trained even for a job as a jailer, no less for one in which they had to use psychology and man-to-man humanity in the treatment of their prisoners. Baker didn't just take away punishment, he instituted educational programs geared to teach an inmate something besides making license plates—instruction that would help ease an ex-felon's reentry into society by providing him with marketable abilities. He brought college education into the prison, making it available to all convicts, not just those few the administration deemed ready to travel outside the institution to attend classes at the College of Santa Fe. He initiated Project Newgate, a program that tutored inmates who wanted to get into the college classes but needed more study to meet the scholastic requirements for entrance.

Rodriguez and his clique had the last word, how-

ever. Baker took over as warden just after the 1968
legislative session ended. It would be ten months before they would meet again to take up the business of
confirming his appointment. In that interim, the press
and legislators heard about the liberal changes Baker
had been making. Knowing their constituency didn't
like politicians who were soft on crime, the legislature
told Baker he was going too fast too soon; the state
couldn't afford the money he was asking them to
spend on Corrections, and therefore they could not
agree to keep him on as warden. They did, however,
agree to give Felix Rodriguez the job.

The inmates' frustration over the reinstitution of the
punishment philosophy of Rodriguez and his clique
boiled over in 1971. In spite of the fact that a grand
jury report in July of that year suggested that the vocational training facilities should be made available to
more inmates, the clique continued their use of these
programs as rewards for good behavior, which meant
the willingness to supply information. And in spite of
the fact that the same grand jury report urged the hiring of a full-time resident psychiatrist "who is particularly trained in the areas of criminal psychology, narcotics counselling, and alcoholism . . ." none was
sought, no less hired. The convicts therefore had no
help and much hindrance in adjusting to the switch
from being treated like humans to being handled like
animals. When the riot at Attica came down in September 1971, they were inspired to raise their own
voices in protest and a month later staged a work
strike that wasn't all together peaceful. Several dormitories were torn apart before it was quelled by
police and tear gas. To Rodriguez's credit, he did later
interview many of the strikers to hear their complaints

about conditions. He was a good enough politician to act on what he heard. In the interest of keeping peace in the prison and the public's eye off his domain, Rodriguez opened up the educational and vocational training to more than just his goody-two-shoes inmates. But others also had incentives for maintaining the status quo: Those who had jobs and were participating in classes, along with those who ran the drug-dealing rackets, didn't want any waves made either and were instrumental in keeping the rest of population quiet during the coming years. Dealing in prison during those days was easy. I, too, had a nice money-making hustle going on, getting marijuana smuggled in and selling it off at a dollar a joint. As long as I didn't get in The Man's way, I knew my operation was safe.

For four more years this went on while Rodriguez and his tight little clique ruled the penitentiary. Then in 1975, just a year after the election of a new progressive Governor and an ambitious Attorney General, their power preserve was ruptured. Attorney General Tony Anaya had been elected to that office on the heels of a man who had brought more than a taint of corruption to it, and he was determined to restore integrity to the position. When allegations of loan sharking, drug trafficking, and bookmaking were made against the prison hospital administrator, Frank Stockham, Anaya launched a full-scale investigation into the matter. Observers in the media considered this move a purely political one because Stockham had just been recommended for a promotion by his friend of many years, the new Governor, Jerry Apodaca. The complaint against Stockham, who was not one of the clique, had been lodged by Rodriguez's top men in response to the Governor's recommendation. The Attorney General's investigation showed, however, that they had done a bit more than simply *file* the complaint, they had in fact framed it through the use of their snitches. The report told the public what we on the inside had always known: that there had indeed been a "clique that has run the penitentiary for a number of years. . . As much as the inmates use one another, they are also being used by some prison officials."⁵ Nor was there any evidence to support the criminal charges leveled against the hospital administrator. Though Stockham admitted that he'd taken drugs from the hospital for his personal use, and that his loose control had made it possible for the inmates to have easy access to drugs, only one allegation was proven:

> It appears Stockham was attempting to assist an inmate secure money from his mother in order to pay gambling debts to other inmates. There was fear for the inmate's safety from the threats of his fellow inmates to whom he owed the money. Despite his humanitarian motives, this action violates penitentiary rules.

Because of this violation, the clique had its way and Stockholm was fired. This didn't take the heat off of them, however. The report went on to say:

> It is the conclusion of the Attorney General's office that each senior corrections and penitentiary administrative official is responsible to some degree for the hasty and unprofessional manner in which the Stockham report was put together and for acting on a report which was of highly questionable reliability. The warden and deputy warden should be each held responsible for failing to

conduct a more thorough and professional investigation and for the use of hopes and promises or the veiled promises, of early parole board, changes in working conditions, or changes in living conditions in the penitentiary to secure false statements.[6]

The report detailed the "investigation" the administration had conducted to make their charges of drug trafficking et al against Stockham, saying it consisted of information from five convicts and one prison employee. "Four of the five received preferential treatment (such as being moved to trustee status or better work detail). All of them testified they knew they would be rewarded for statements made against Stockham and punished if they did not give derogatory statements." The Attorney General concluded the report by noting that though drug-trafficking was not found in Frank Stockham's case, there was unchecked entry of heroin, cocaine, cash, and liquor into the prison; and that the Stockham affair "has highlighted the manner in which corrections and penitentiary officials can manipulate employees and inmates to serve their own selfish interests."[7]

As a result, the corrections secretary was fired; Warden Rodriguez, a deputy warden, the chief security officer, and an associate warden were removed from their jobs inside the penitentiary. These four, however, were transferred to other positions within the state's Department of Corrections, where they all remained in top management well beyond the 1980 riot.

With the ousting of the main members of the clique, the inmates had high hopes that the new Governor, the first Chicano to be elected to the state's highest office in fifty-four years, was going to change the quality of prison life. Those hopes soared when his newly appointed corrections secretary hired as his administrative aid, an ex-hardcore con, a man who'd spent twelve years in the penitentiary, two of them on Death Row, on a first-degree murder conviction that had been commuted to life when the state's death penalty was found unconstitutional. He was the only inmate I've seen in all my years in the pen who used his time not only to educate himself but to totally transform his way of thinking. Unfortunately, the hiring of this ex-con was the only progressive prison event in Governor Apodaca's term. It hadn't been a bed of roses under the Rodriguez clan, but what was to come made it look like it had been.

The new warden was not the great white hope everyone expected. Ralph Aaron, an ex-federal warden with thirty years in corrections under his belt, came in with the hard-line attitude that the institution had gone to hell and he was going to take control because the inmates were running the place. Unlike Rodriguez, who would at least give a con a fair hearing, Aaron treated the inmates as if they were lucky to be breathing. As sparsely as the educational projects had been made available to prisoners under Rodriguez, under Warden Aaron they wre practically nil. All programs that took an inmate outside the prison were closed down. Project Newgate folded because no one had bothered to seek funding for it.[7a] Gone now were the incentives—even the illegal ones—that had kept inmates in line for the past four years. The Attorney General's report on the Rodriguez clique had brought the state police in to check the drug flow into the prison. This cut down on the rackets, though it didn't entirely eradicate them; they had, after all, been flourishing during the old regime, and many of the prison personnel who had been involved in them were still working in the institution. "Not only were the guards aware, for example, of the narcotics trafficking," ex-Attorney General Tony Anaya told a reporter, "but some of the guards and some of the higher-ups had to be actually participating in the actual trafficking itself. It simply could not go on to the extent that it was going on without the actual involvement by officials."[8]

Though Warden Aaron's clampdown and tight security measures made it difficult to get drugs and make a comfortable prison living from their sale, his attempts to clean up the penitentiary were frustrated at every turn. Answering a question by a newsperson as to whether he found that guards had been bringing drugs into the prison during his administration, Aaron said, "Yes, we found there were several. We had a problem. We talked with officials downtown about it. I was told at a later date, not too long before I resigned, . . . that, 'Don't worry about it; particularly if the guy was Chicano, you're not going to get him convicted.'"[9]

It was this, together with the fact that his strict ideas about security procedures were not being carried out (years later he told of watching an officer leave a meeting about security regulations, walk down the corridor, and casually slide open and leave open every grill he passed through), that made Aaron quit just six months after he started. However, he managed to hand-pick his successor.

Clyde Malley's fetish for security was as strong as his predecessor's, but he was as ineffectual in changing the laxness of the guards as Aaron had been. In fact, during the seventeen months the two of them shared the office of warden at the penitentiary, there were nineteen escapes, more than there had been in the past ten years. The frustrated Malley attributed one of those escapes to "a complete breakdown of security, established procedures, misinformation, lack of responsible leadership, and general chaos. In thirty years in corrections, I have never witnessed such a total breakdown of basic prison practices."[10]

If this carelessness was the guards' way of saying they weren't satisfied with the conditions they were being dished out as underpaid and undertrained corrections officers, the inmates, too, found a way of expressing their displeasure over the severe restrictions placed on them. Not only had the outside educational programs been discontinued; in his attempt at greater security, Malley had removed all convicts from their administrative positions in the remaining programs, returning them to the idleness that was fast becoming the most abundant occupation in the institution. The convict's mind is never idle, however, since thinking is one of the few rights that can't be taken from him.

During the spring of 1976, the residents at Santa Fe spent their free time scheming on ways to get the administration to change their tune. They knew the only effective means of doing that was to catch the public's attention; this meant staging some kind of uprising to protest conditions, which were intolerable from every point of view. Besides Malley's oppressive regime, the institution was infested with rats and cockroaches, the toilets didn't work, and the food was, as usual, bad. Back and forth through the vents went talk about what kind of action to take. It was decided that the entire population would stage a sit-down strike while the warden had a chance to look over their list of grievances and demands. They were agreed that if the administration didn't show signs of giving in on at least some points on that list, they would launch an all-out riot and tear the prison apart. The strike leaders wrote up their tabulation of gripes and remedies and passed the word through the grapevine that they were ready to go.

On the morning of Flag Day, Monday, June 14, 1976, everyone remained in the housing units and refused to go to work or to meals until their complaints were answered. By noon the administration sent word: "We're tired of your game; you either go to the mess hall tonight or we're coming in to lock you up." No compromises, no mention of grievances. The inmates didn't budge; and The Man did as he promised, locking all cellblock residents in their "houses," and closing the gates to the dormitory units. Those in the cellblocks couldn't do much damage, but the five-hundred inmates housed in the dormitories carried out their plan and tore their units apart. Four of the prison's five dorms were demolished before the riot was brought under control by guards with tear gas. No one was taken hostage, no one was seriously hurt, and none of the grievances or demands were even discussed. All that was accomplished by this outbreak was more punishment. After the tear gassing, six hundred inmates were taken, twenty or thirty at a time, and forced to strip naked and stand in the main corridor while lines of guards and prison personnel on either side questioned them to find out who the strike leaders were. Of course no one talked; no convict was going to snitch in front of his fellows, and the administration had to know this. The interrogation could only have been designed for the purpose of humiliation and retribution, as was the axe-handle gauntlet that followed. As the buck-naked inmates were made to run between the two lines of corrections officers on their way to the gymnasium, they were smacked on the butt, the head, the back, and the arms by those who wielded large axe handles. Some convicts were hurt seriously enough to warrant being sent to the infirmary for stitches; others suffered broken knees and elbows, and all suffered yet another loss of self-esteem.

One of these axe-handle wielders was a member of the church. He was hated by the inmates because he catered to the "short eyes," those who were child molesters and sex offenders, the most despised convicts in any prison. They were, in fact, the only men who attended services in his chapel. He was a sight, going around to all the dormitories after this axe-handle scene, preaching a hell-and-brimstone sermon to excuse his actions. He'd done it for God, of course, and everyone deserved everything that was happening to them, bad conditions and all; all he and the prison administration were trying to do, he explained, was "get the devil out of you." From that day on, he became known as the "Axehandle". During the 1980 riot, the convicts gave him his payback by burning down a chapel.

Warden Malley never made an effort to talk to inmates about their complaints. His only concern was finding and punishing the strike leaders. Those he believed to be the instigators he placed in Segregation and kept them there for months, even years, according to the Attorney General's report on the incident.[11] Others were transferred out of the prison to another state to insure the tight control the security-oriented warden needed but never achieved. He offered no incentives to lure the inmates into good behavior; no reward, only punishment. Being locked up was such a common occurrence that the convicts began to use it to their own advantage. It not only tended to enhance their tough-guy image, but many looked forward to a stay in Cellblock 3, preferring to finish out their sentences in the privacy of a cell rather than in population, where violence, rape, and overcrowding was increasing. And of course, escapes continued. As one inmate expressed it, "Why is someone willing to go over a fence right by a tower, risking his life, knowing that they'll shoot him if they spot him? . . . Because he's so frustrated with this place, doesn't see no way out, can't work towards his freedom, that he decides it's better to be shot, it's better to be killed than to remain here."[12]

In 1978, after little more than a year on the job, Warden Malley quit in disgust. He had failed to grasp the fact that control wasn't the only way to deal with human beings. Maybe his thirty years in corrections had jaded him so thoroughly that he'd forgotten it was humanity he was dealing with. "We only stay in control of prisons to the degree that the prison population as a whole sees our administration as fair, humane, somewhat reasonable, and something they can understand. When we reach the point where a large number of prisoners see our administration as something other than that, then we have the potential for anything," commented another veteran of corrections, Lloyd Patterson, thirty years with the California prison system, aptly, but too late. "I think most people who work in prisons . . . lose sight and say, 'Hey, we are in control. We got you guys, and we've got all the gas and the sticks and guns that we need to control you." . . . You get that idea and you're in trouble."[13]

Perhaps it was the state's recognition that a more humane administering of the prison was needed that made them appoint two gentler though less qualified men to succeed Malley. Neither the acting warden, who filled the bill while a permanent man was being sought, nor the final selection had the experience to handle the job with authority. The highest position Warden Jerry Griffin had held in corrections before taking over the top post at Santa Fe was superintendent of the Roswell Center—a minimum security institution that included community contact and community release—hardly the background to be of assistance to him in this violent maximum security penitentiary. In the year and a few months these two relatively weak administrators filled the top position at the penitentiary, the prison fell into the full control of the clique once again. Deputy Warden Robert Montoya, who arrived at the institution under Warden Aaron in 1975, was now the leader, at least on the inside. The Corrections Department itself was in turmoil, having experienced as many correction secretaries as the prison had wardens. The only firm voice in the department was that of the still-powerful original kingpin, Felix Rodriguez. Many who'd worked under Rodriguez when he was warden remained at the penitentiary; together with the deputy warden, they reinstituted the power of the Santa Fe Eleven and the effective insanity of the snitch circuit.

By far the most hated member of this clique was a lieutenant nicknamed Greeneyes. Snitches weren't Greeneyes' cup of brew; his priority was playing games with an inmate's mind. He would go out of his way to make trouble for a convict, call him degrading names to his face, challenge him to talk back, throw him in the Hole if he didn't, then get the goon squad to tear gas and beat him. I've seen him harass an inmate so many times I still have nightmares about him. Once when I was in lockup in Cellblock 3, there was a Chicano a few cells down who knew his family was visiting that day. Greeneyes, who was on duty, had already told him to get dressed. After waiting an hour and still not being called again, the dude yelled over to Greeneyes, "Hey, you told me an hour ago to get ready, how come?"

"You better shut your mouth," Greeneyes answered. "I'm tired of hearing it. You open it again, you won't have any visiting privilege, today or any day."

What could the inmate do but sit and fume in silence. When another forty-five minutes went by, he lost his cool. The fact that he'd been told to get ready meant his visitor was already there and waiting. "Hey, what's the delay with my visit?" he shouted again.

Greeneyes got up and called to the guard in the control booth outside the tier to come inside. When he did, the two of them walked over to the convict's cell, cranked open the door, and pulled him out. "Okay, smartass, we're taking you where you can scream all you want. You won't have to worry about your visits for a while." When a convict is taken to the Hole, he has to wait thirty days before he's eligible to have visitors again. While he screamed and pleaded, they dragged the guy down to the basement, stripped him naked, and shoved him into the dark maximum detention unit, all because he had the audacity to be concerned about his weekly one-hour chance to talk to someone who actually cared about him, someone who could, for sixty minutes out of his endless monotonous time, make him feel like a human being.

One day I was standing in line to get canteen supplies when Greeneyes pulled someone out of the line and made him go back to his unit without buying anything. That meant the con had to spend the week without the cigarettes, coffee, Kool-Aid, and snacks that make the days go by with at least a modicum of pleasure. His great crime was that he had dropped something and stepped a few feet out of formation to pick it up. It's small things like this that build and make a man hate.

Many grievances were filed against Greeneyes, but nothing ever came of them. He was, after all, a longstanding member of the clique. The administration agreed he might be a little hard on the inmates, but they backed his action and let him continue. He was so despised that during the 1980 riot the negotiators offered to give up three of their hostages if they could have Greeneyes instead.

The intelligence officer was another long-time member of the clique. His job was "to collect, collate, and evaluate intelligence information affecting the safe operation of the penitentiary,"[14] and he achieved that goal by relying heavily on his snitch lines. The trouble was that he believed anything he was told and never bothered to investigate before he acted on a tip and had an inmate locked up. Consequently, a lot of grudges between inmates were settled by channelling bogus information through this intelligence officer. Informants itching for better jobs or transfers to the honor unit knew they could feed him a lie and collect their reward. As long as it was plausible, this officer would buy it. Many a convict, innocent of the charge, has been locked up in Cellblock 3, sometimes for as long as six months, on another inmate's unproven word. I could never figure whether this man was stupid, lazy, or thought every convict was a badass, anyway. Two weeks before the riot, he was transferred out of the penitentiary, but to another position in the Corrections Department.

Many of the guards, too, developed their own snitch lines, thereby earning for themselves the promotion given by the administration when an officer was deemed "attentive to prisoners' needs."[15] In reality, this was a power game that was dangerous, sometimes fatal, to inmates and never answered any of their "needs," only those of the clique. When they saw a convict they wanted to turn into one of their snitches, usually a young, new inmate, a guard would approach him. At the start, the kid wouldn't go for it. Then came the convincing. They'd throw him in Cellblock 5 with the hardcore cons who'd beat and rape him. When it was all over, the captain or lieutenant would come back and offer him their protection: "You do what we need you to do and we'll keep those guys off your back." If he still refused, they'd put a false "snitch jacket" on him, their favorite payback to convicts they either didn't like or who wouldn't work with them: They'd let the word slip out to population that the con had been talking to them, knowing the other inmates would jump to the conclusion that it was true. Enraged as they were by their circumstances, most convicts were happy to have some scapegoat to vent their anger on. They wouldn't sit down and figure out whether the dude really snitched on someone or whether The Man had something against him. They'd make the assumption that the sonofabitch had been talking. Then the guy was in trouble, with fifty convicts ready to get on his case with fists and shanks. He couldn't fight fifty men, so he had to leave population and stay locked up in the protection unit with a reputation he hadn't earned.

It's true that only men with basically weak constitutions, who didn't have the stamina to stand up to the punishment The Man would dish out, wound up snitching. But as much as the convicts gave the snitch a hard time, it was still understood that half the blame went to these upholders of the law, these so-called rehabilitators of the criminal mind who used their position of power to manipulate and intimidate an inmate into betraying his friends. Even The Man had no respect for an informer, nor did he offer him solace or reward when his usefulness was ended. Once a snitch was found out by the rest of population, it was a lonely life. If he was lucky enough to avoid getting killed, his name was forever mud. He had to spend the rest of his time locked up day and night knowing he was despised by everyone, guards and inmates alike.

Like the snitches, Deputy Warden Montoya had the distinction of being despised by both inmates and guards. The officers would openly complain to us about him, mainly because he treated them as badly as he treated convicts. If a guard wasn't playing footsies with the clique, Montoya would give him the royal shaft by shifting him to tower duty or some equally obnoxious work detail. In some cases, Montoya would make things so intolerable for the officer, he'd be forced to resign, as happened in one well-publicized incident involving a twenty-seven-year-old newcomer to the penitentiary. The way Bruce Podlesny told the story, he saw a window one day with broken glass in it, "just hanging there, splintered," and knocked it out to prevent someone from cutting themselves or even using the glass as a weapon. Someone, no doubt a friend of the clique, reported him for breaking the window, and Podlesny was called down to Montoya's office to explain. According to Podlesny, Montoya tagged him a psycho and said he didn't believe the officer had broken off already-splintered glass from just four or five panes; he believed he'd actually smashed all thirty-five panes of glass that made up the window. Montoya gave him a choice: resign, in which case his employment record would remain clean and he wouldn't have to pay for the windows, or be fired and pay for them. Podlesny resigned, but $157 was still deducted from his last paycheck as payment for the windows he insisted he never broke. Montoya denied Podlesny's story, saying that he'd never accused the officer of being a psycho or of window breaking. "We counseled him in reference to the window breaking," he told reporters, but he didn't recall "the circumstances surrounding his termination or resignation." Nor did he know anything about the guard's final check and the deduction made on it because, he said, "my concern is programs."[16]

A group of guards, however, backed up Podlesny's version of the event, using it to exemplify their own dissatisfaction with working under Montoya. "You have your little fiefdoms out there. Employees who make mistakes on the job are disciplined if they're on the outs with the power structure, but get off scot-free if they're tied to a clique."[17] They were complaining, they explained to the reporter, so they could get the public's attention and induce the Corrections Department to give the officers more training and more

chance for advancement. Only 30 percent of the corrections staff had received formal classroom training.
Even in Rodriguez's time, warden training had been
nonexistent. By 1979, in fact, there was more formal
training offered than ever before. Because the prison
was understaffed, though, few newcomers and no old-
timers could be spared from duty to attend these
classes. In addition to this formal study, new officers
were supposed to receive a basic orientation during
their first week on duty, but some guards reported that
the program was little more than a tour of the penitentiary. "If you're lucky, a fellow officer will show you
what you have to do if he has time," one guard told the
Attorney General's investigators.[18] Another veteran
officer told them that "his best initial instruction on
key and grill handling came from inmates."[19]

The man in charge of keeping the corrections
officers on their toes was another old-timer clique
member, as careless in his treatment of inmates as he
was lax in enforcing security procedures. During his
seventeen years on the rise from guard to superintendent of correctional security he'd proven himself to be
one of the least sympathetic officers in the penitentiary. He never took the time to talk to an inmate
regardless of the problem at hand, and if he had it
would have had to be a fellow Chicano because he
could barely speak English. It was during his term as
security chief that so many escapes occurred and the
1980 riot exploded. If anyone had been concerned
about how the prison was being managed, they would
have seen he wasn't taking care of business. Only after
the riot did the laziness he allowed begin to surface. In
the words of one of the officers under his command,
"For sixteen hours a day and on weekends, the place

was run by captains who made a lot of accommodations, causing rampant inconsistencies. . . . At least half the time when I walked into the place in the morning . . . we were not flying the colors. . . . Now, you may not be able to relate that to basic security procedures, but I do. . . . Something is done every day all the time because it is supposed to be done."[20] This old-timer was removed from his job after the 1980 riot, and another veteran of corrections in New Mexico, one of the original clique members with a penchant for putting the goon squad on unruly inmates, took over the position.

Given this lack of supervision, the guards had the power to act on their own and lock up convicts for any infraction they could dream up, and they dreamed up some humdingers. Inmates were sent to lockup for walking down the wrong side of the corridor, for lying on their bunks after morning wake-up call, or for taking crackers out of the kitchen; one prisoner was sent to lockup because he'd cut his finger and smashed it while unloading trash in the dump site. Lockup was so prevalent a punishment there was triple bunking in Cellblock 3, while in Cellblock 4 Protection, there were two to a cell because the snitch circuits were so carelessly used that informants were being found out as soon as they fingered someone.

None of this helped to calm the mounting rage of the inmates, nor was there any help from top management. The warden was never available to anyone, and Deputy Warden Montoya was a lost cause as far as the convicts were concerned. This man was never straight with a convict. Someone would stop him and ask for a job change or say he needed to talk to him about something important, and Montoya would say, "Sure, I'll get to you this afternoon," or, "I'll call you in the morning." That would be the end of it; the inmate would never hear from him. A week later he'd see Montoya again and ask what happened. Montoya would look at him like he didn't know what he was talking about and tell him he never said any such thing. He demonstrated no interest in the well-being of the prisoners. His whole framework was one of force and security gained through the fear he and his officers could evoke in a man. Many of the prisoners felt that Montoya was blatantly prejudiced against whites and blacks, especially those who belonged to the cliques. Numbers of the inmates believed that he would lock up members of the Aryan Brotherhood on the slightest provocation, and they felt that he had even less use for the Black Muslims. On the other hand, it seemed to them that he'd bend over backwards for his brother Chicanos. . . ." When six Chicanos jumped one white inmate, beating and raping him, and the white con turned them in, Montoya had no choice but to lock them up. The next day, though, he gave them more slack than he'd ever given a white or black. He called them into his office and asked if they'd done what they were accused of. Naturally, the six said no. "Six against one, that's good enough for me," Montoya told them. "I can't see any reason to hold you guys in lockup any more." They were free, but a few months later he had no qualms about holding a group of whites and one black in lockup for weeks in spite of a report from one of his own officers that there were no grounds to do so. These weren't the only actions of Montoya's that triggered the February riot. A few jailhouse lawyers had filed lawsuits to secure improvements in certain prison conditions, the Black Muslim court order being the result of one. After waiting two and a half years for the courts to take some action or another, a "partial consent decree" was signed in the fall of 1979 ordering the implementation of increased mail and visitation privileges. Montoya took his time instituting these new policies, infuriating the convicts, many of whom were clique leaders, who'd worked so hard and waited so long to see the fruits of their efforts.[20a]

As if all of this wasn't enough to make the prison blow apart, there were the insidious practices of the psychological services unit. Dr. Mark Orner, the psychologist heading the unit, was also a member of the clique. His actions during his time at the penitentiary earned him the animosity of the inmates and caused them to burn down the psych unit with particular vigor during the riot. As a former inmate told reporters, "The overkill and butchery you saw during the riot was one of rage, and the rage was from the stress in that prison. And it's my opinion that the psychological services unit added to that stress more than it reduced the rage."[21] Like the other clique members, Dr. Orner played one inmate off against the other. In addition, his evaluations of a convict had a great amount of pull with the parole board, and he used that fact to gather information; if a man didn't tell him what he wanted to know, Orner would tell the board the con wasn't ready for society yet. Since, as a psychologist, he was thought to have a special talent for understanding human nature, the board went along with his opinion 99¾ percent of the time.

The psychological services unit was started in 1973. Most of the convicts thought it was a big joke and a waste of money. They had no respect for Orner, no trust in him or his counsellors. They knew Orner's staff reported back to him, and they weren't about to unburden their feelings so he could ruin their records if he didn't like what he heard. Besides, when new inmates would mistakenly go to the counsellors for help in handling the jungle they were facing for the first time, the advice they were given was the same they would have gotten from a guard or administrator: Go on back and tough it out. Even if Orner and his staff had been willing to honestly work with the problems a man faces in the penitentiary, where would they begin? Convicts aren't about to unload to The Man when their entire day-to-day existence deals in secret plots to get around the administration; nor are they likely to confide in a psychologist who was a member of the punishment-dealing segregation committee, as Orner was. The psychological problems in prison can't be solved by talking about them anyway; it's prison itself that breeds paranoia, depression, and aggressive feelings.

Dr. Orner was only a doctor of psychology. Though he denies it, reports always managed to circulate that he was strongly opposed to the hiring of a psychiatrist. When a team of forensic health care consultants for the American Civil Liberties Union came to the penitentiary in 1979 to inspect the medical facilities, a psychiatrist in the group quoted Dr. Orner as telling him, "'I'll leave if a psychiatrist comes here.' . . . Orner told me that he had spent seven years building up his psychological services staff and that he did not want any outsiders threatening his position or his staff's credibility."[22]

According to this team of consultants, Dr. Orner and his psychological services unit never supplied adequate care for the mentally ill who made up 10 percent of the prison population. Because these psychotic inmates were thrown into dormitories with the main-

stream of convicts, they were cause or victim of
"nearly half the violent incidents within the penitentiary"[23] and usually would end up in the Hole for
indefinite periods of time without the benefit of the
therapy or tranquilizers their condition demanded.
What little counselling they did receive consisted of
one of Orner's aids walking by their windowless cell
door asking a brief, "How's everything today?" Dr.
Orner and the prison's medical director both had "anti-
pathy to psychiatry, psychiatrists, and the use of
psychotropic medication, including major tranquilizers,"[24] the latter being standard treatment for
psychotic and schizophrenic disorders. The forensic
unit of the state hospital in Las Vegas, New Mexico,
where these mentally ill convicts should have gone
except for the fact that the facility did not have enough
room for them, wrote to this team of medical consultants "that prisoners arrive from the penitentiary in a
catatonic state and it is obvious to them they are re-
ceiving no treatment."[25] They cited as example one
prisoner who was considered "a raving lunatic" and
transferred to Las Vegas. Through the use of Lox-
itane, an antipsychotic, he reached what doctors described as a "stable remission," stable enough for him
to be sent back to the penitentiary. When he returned
there, he was given no medication, even though it had
been prescribed, and "soon became floridly psychotic
again."[26]

Some of those inmates whose mental balance went
awry managed to escape their suffering by killing
themselves. Between 1968 and 1977, there were seven
successful suicides in the prison, and between June
1978 and May 1979, several suicide attempts were re-
corded. Those who tried but didn't succeed were
placed in lockup or in a special dungeon hole near the

gas chamber in the basement of Cellblock 5, where no guards were stationed and no one could hear their constant screams to be set free. Others who were more violently suicidal were treated to one of the most bizarre procedures in prison history, a plaster body cast from neck to ankles with holes for defacation and urination. This restraint was developed in 1978 by the penitentiary's medical director as an alternative to drug therapy. As he explained to the team of forensic consultants, he thought it was "probably more humane to physically restrain people"[27] than to make them suffer the aftereffects of some tranquilizers. His premise is dimmed, however, by the fact that Thorazine had to be forced down a fit-throwing convict's throat to get him to submit to being placed in a body cast. Dr. Orner spoke about his use of these casts at a meeting of the American Medical Association's Conference on Health Services in Correctional Facilities in November 1979, explaining that he was using body casts as a method of crisis intervention. "And he did it in almost a bragging tone—he sounded like he thought it was terrific," one listener, an attorney with the New York Legal Aid Society, commented. "I asked him how he got people into it, considering that they would be supposedly violent people in some kind of episode, and he said that if it took six officers, eight officers, it didn't matter how many it took to hold the guy down."[28]

According to an interview with an ex-inmate of the Penitentiary of New Mexico who was placed in a body cast in the summer of 1979, it was Thorazine that subdued him.

> I was brought down to the hospital in handcuffs, and thrown off into the strip cell a number of times. Finally they upped and stuffed me off in

that ol' cast situation. . . . But before they did that, they poured Thorazine down my throat. Held my jaws right there, and just poured it right in my face because I didn't want to take it. Well . . . after I got in that full body cast, I busted all out of that, man, because I was hysterical. Scared. Somebody's trying to kill me. . . .[29]

A psychologist from an east coast state mental health unit who treated this man before he'd gone into the Land of Enchantment's prison told reporters he "seriously deteriorated while in the New Mexico state pen. He came back much worse than when he went out there. He returned totally schizophrenic."[30]

Punishment was the prison's going treatment for insanity. When a psychotic, mentally disturbed convict was brought before the segregation committee, which included psychologist Marc Orner, the man would be treated like he'd done something wrong, sent to lockup or stripped naked and thrown in the Hole or, worse yet, the dungeon cell near the gas chamber; all his privileges were gone—no canteen, no visiting, no television. Five of the inmates killed in the February 1980 riot were mentally ill. One was Juan Sanchez, who died in the Hole, where he'd been locked up. Two were in the protection unit, Cellblock 4, one in Cellblock 3, and the other was new enough to the prison to still be living in population. They were killed because none of the prisoners understood their insanity any more than the administration did.

"Do you know why it's so hard to treat mentally disturbed prisoners at the state pen?" a former New Mexico prison psychologist rhetorically asked, and then aptly answered: "Because it's the institution that has a character disorder."[31]

VII

The dude that sent me to the penitentiary for life, someone who's sittin' over there doin' six months while I'm sittin' here doin' life and I got a chance to get to that dude? You bet I'm gonna break my back to get to him. The guy they burned all to pieces with a cuttin' torch, well he deserved that a hundred times more. Whoever did that ought to get a medal pinned on his chest. A baby raper and a child molester, that's a sick individual and he's got anything comin' that anybody does to him.

—Inmate, PENITENTIARY OF NEW MEXICO[1]

5:00 A.M., Saturday, February 2, 1980. The fire in the psychological services unit was roaring. Rioters had turned the blowtorch to the unit to put the finishing touch on its destruction. Just above it, in the old Men's dormitory, where I was, the smoke was getting so thick we began to think we wouldn't get out alive. Flames were licking up the stairwell, the only exit, and the intense heat from the fire below made it impossible to stand on the floor. Finally someone remembered the band practice room was just behind the dormitory. Using the metal beds as battering rams, we managed to knock through a wall into the room and save our lives. There were windows there which we smashed open, each of us stationing ourselves by a broken pane and breathing in fresh air.

The band room overlooked the front gate of the penitentiary. We could see that police had already arrived, and over the two-way radio a rioter had given us, we'd been hearing that Deputy Warden Montoya was there also. We tried to contact him, but it took a while. "The smoke is real bad up here," we told him when we finally got his attention. "It's beginning to get to a lot of men. The fire's so hot downstairs it looks like the floor might collapse, and if it does, there's fifty or sixty men here that burn to death."

"There's nothing we can do to help you," Montoya answered. "None of the administration is coming into the penitentiary. The only thing you can do is find some way out on your own."

"But we can't get out; the only way out is blocked by flames and smoke. No one can get through."

Someone who thought they could get the point across better grabbed the radio. "Man, we're burnin' up. You gotta do something or everyone up here's gonna be cremated; can't you bring us some chains at least, so we can jerk these windows loose and jump out?"

"That's your problem," came the reply. "You'll have to get out the best way you can." End of communication.

Fortunately some of the blacks next door in Cellhouse 6 were interested in using the band room as a command post and decided to help us. Breaking the emergency glass in the hallway, they took the fire hose, hooked it up to a faucet in the janitorial closet between the two units, and drenched the stairway. When the flames were subdued, rioters wearing gas masks made their way upstairs through the smoke to see what they could do for us. They offered the masks to anyone who wanted to make their way down to the gymnasium, but there were no takers. By this time the open windows and the dousing of the fire had cleared the air somewhat and we decided not to leave. Aside from our wariness about the sanity of the rioters, there were a few men in the dorm guilty of sex crimes who felt they might be harmed if recognized by some drugged, raving con.

The blacks set up their command post in the band room, with its full-on view of the front of the prison and the activities of the police. They had several two-way radios, and to distract ourselves from the smoke and heat we paid attention to the transmissions between the riot negotiators and the Man outside. From these we learned that the rioters had taken a blowtorch to the grill that blocked the protection unit and the empty Cellblock 5 from the main corridor.

"Hey, *ese*," the Chicano voice said to someone calling himself Chopper One. "We're just now starting to cut the grill. When we get through, we're gonna burn into 5 and see if there are any more torches in there, or whatever else we can use when we get into Protection. We're going down after the snitches, gonna kill us some of those motherfuckers, man."

"Okay," Chopper One answered. "You get it open, you let me know. I wanna get that snitchin' bastard that sent me into lockup for six months; send him home to his mama."

For the next hour and a half we heard them talking back and forth about their progress.

"Well, how're you doin?" Chopper One called to ask at one point. "How long is it gonna take you guys to get those bars cut?"

"Well, we're still at it; I think we're runnin' low on oxygen. Someone will have to go down and get another bottle."

Deputy Warden Montoya and his crew outside were also picking up these transmissions and knew that a massacre of snitches was imminent. They knew, too, that it was going to take the rioters some time to cut through the two sets of bars; time enough for police to come in by the sally port area in the rear of the prison, enter Cellblock 4 by a back entrance, to which they were supposed to have keys in the guard tower in front, and lead the ninety-six men in the unit out to safety. Even if they didn't have the keys to the back door, there was a garage in the sally port area where other cutting torches were kept. They could have attempted what the rioters were doing and cut the door open. But they didn't. Later, prison administrators would explain to investigators that the set of keys in the tower was imcomplete; there were keys to the back door of the cellblock but none to the grill allowing entrance into the cell area. Whether it was a matter of missing keys or missing motivation is a question that will be debated for years, both privately and in courts hearing the claims of families that their sons, brothers, and husbands were killed due to the negligence of prison authorities.

The deputy warden and superintendent of correctional security had arrived at the main gatehouse in front of the prison shortly after the riot began, for they both lived on the grounds. Warden Jerry Griffin, who also lived on the prison reservation, joined them shortly thereafter. The security chief armed the tower officers with riot guns as one of his first tactics, instructing them to fire on anyone attempting to escape. This proved an unnecessary move. The inmates made it clear in their first radio communication with these officials that they weren't going to try to escape; they were holding out for a meeting with the news media and Governor Bruce King. But the rioters warned that if the National Guard or state police tried to rush the institution, they would kill their hostages, and they put Captain Roybal on the radio to repeat and confirm their intention.

The three administrators talked it over and agreed to negotiate the release of the hostages rather than attempt to retake the penitentiary. By common consent Montoya was designated negotiator; he'd recently returned from San Francisco, where he'd taken a timely course in crisis intervention and hostage situations. His strategy was to keep the rioters from talking to the Governor and the warden, feeling their position might force them to yield to the rioters' demands. Setting up first in his car and then in the gatehouse, Montoya used a handset radio to carry on his talks with the inmate negotiators. He conducted himself in the manner learned at "hostage school,"[2] alternating between soothing and harsh tones. Most of his dialogues were with Chopper One, but the person behind that name changed several times throughout the negotiations. So many inmates had two-way radios that it was hard to decipher what was being said or who was really in the position to speak for the rioters. Montoya's radio was also picking up communications from sheriff's officers who had arrived on the scene, so that many inmate transmissions were lost in the confusion. When he finally demanded that the officers stop using the radios, the babble cleared enough for him to figure out that regardless of the change in person behind the name, Chopper One was the main negotiating station. Most inmate demands made during these early hours remained consistent throughout the uprising. The prison was not to be rushed or the hostages would be killed. They wanted to talk with the Governor, the warden, Deputy Secretary of Corrections Felix Rodriguez, and the news media. They wanted a public forum to air their complaints about "poor food, overcrowding, mismanagement at the penitentiary, and inadequate recreation."[3] And they asked for the resignations of the administrators they most despised: the deputy warden himself; Associate Warden Adelaido Martinez; the superintendent of correctional security, Manuel Koroneos and Lieutenant Benito Gonzales, known better by inmates as Greeneyes.

It wasn't until ex-Warden Rodriguez arrived that action on the convicts' behalf began. A hose was dragged to the main entrance of the prison to try and combat the fires, though it did little good; and wounded prisoners were allowed to be brought out for treatment. This netted a reward for the administration. The helpful inmates who'd hidden Officer Herman Gallegos in a dormitory at the start of the riot smuggled him past rioters and through the main entrance by dressing him in a prison uniform and arming him with a pipe. Rodriguez was fair but firm. He demanded to know how many hostages were being held and their names. A threat came back across the radio—"If you don't start negotiating pretty soon, these guards are going to get wasted. Captain Roybal will be the first one to pop out of the door dead." Rodriguez countered that if there were no assurances the hostages were still alive he would order the SWAT team inside the penitentiary. "And if that happens," he said, "it's going to be worse than Attica. Kill one of my officers and we'll come in and kill every one of you."

By now the entire penitentiary was surrounded by state police, sheriff's officers and the Sante Fe SWAT team. The Governor had been notified of the riot, and the National Guard was on its way. Meanwhile everyone's radio sets were buzzing with transmissions about the progress of those torching through the grill to Cellblock 4 and threats against the snitches' lives. "All them guys in Cellblock 4 that you've been using," someone broadcast directly to Deputy Warden Montoya, "well, I've got some of them in the sack just in case you don't cooperate. Eyewitnesses that you call the snitches over here. . .they are going to start getting shanked."[4] That killing of the men in Cellblock 4 would occur, these administrators had no doubt. They knew the men in Cellblock 3 had been released; they'd seen them moving up and down the hallways through the windows. But Montoya's newly learned hostage strategy held. No police or staff members were to go near the prison; the major objective was to keep the hostages from being killed. If ninety-six convicts faced being slaughtered, it clearly was of less consequence and only an extension of the public's attitude toward a person convicted of committing a crime.

7:00 A.M., daybreak, Ground-hog Day. Through the billowing smoke that shadowed the sunrise, the guard manning the south tower spotted an inmate crawling out of a window in Unit E, waving a white towel.

When the sirens screaming through the front gates of the penitentiary stopped, he could hear the man yelling, "We want to surrender, we want to surrender." The officer cocked his gun and aimed it at the convict before he leaned out the tower window and answered, "Okay, put your hands on top of your head and lay down on your stomach." The inmate did as told. The men in E-l, the semi-protection unit, had managed to forge an opening in a window with the pipe wrench Joe Madrid died providing them. The guard used his bullhorn to address the men still inside the dormitory. "Come out one at a time, with your hands on your head, and get down on your stomachs." The hole was big enough for only one man at a time anyway; in twenty minutes, all eighty-seven residents had crawled through it and were lying face down on the cold ground outside. They were the first of hundreds of convicts who would run from the insanity inside the prison during the next thirty hours.

The inmates in the full protection unit, Cellblock 4, didn't have such luck. As the men in E-l found freedom, the rioters wielding the cutting torch succeeded in melting through the last hinge of the protection unit grill. Thirty minutes before they'd gotten into Cellblock 5, which was undergoing renovation, and found two more acetyline torches. They'd been left by the construction crew in spite of the fact that two weeks after the December escape of eleven inmates a memo had been sent to the superintendent of security by two guards suggesting that these tools be removed from the institution each day. Later the security chief would say he never saw that memo. These torches now became instruments of torture.

Wearing bandanas pulled up over their faces and ski

hats pulled over their hair, the rioters ran through the opened grill up and down the catwalks of each tier, yelling, "We're comin' after you bastards, we're gonna kill you sorry motherfuckers." They were specific about who they wanted, however. They went straight for the guard station where the picture roster of everyone in the cellblock was kept. Once they found the cell numbers of the men they were after, they divided into groups, roaming the three tiers until they found them.

Getting their marks out of the cell wasn't so easy. When they realized the door to the cellblock was being torched, those in the unit who thought there was a good chance they'd be on the most wanted list began taking security measures. They made smoke bombs of their mattresses, tearing them open, stuffing them with toilet paper, and setting them a fire, hoping that when the rioters broke in, the catwalk would be so thick with smoke they'd be forced out or at least slowed down until help could be gotten. But they weren't slowed, and help never came. The men in Protection were prepared for that eventuality, too. Lifting their beds on end, they jammed the legs into the door rail to keep it from being cranked open, tying bedsheets around the door and the bars of the cell to further insure their safety. Then they armed themselves with chair and table legs and waited for the onslaught.

While bands of masked inmates went looking for the objects of their wrath, taking blowtorches to cut through the barricaded doors, others freed their friends. A black contingent was particularly anxious to get the Black Muslim minister out before the bloodshed began. Because so many inmates had jammed their doors, the lever on the main control board that released the locking device to his cell was stuck. Since his friends couldn't therefore merely crank his door open, they had to get one of the cutting torches and burn through the hinges. When he was free, he immediately cautioned the rioters not to harass the blacks in the unit; he was going to take them out with him. Whites and Chicanos agreed. Though the Aryan Brotherhood's threats on the black leader's life had caused the administration to place the Muslim in Protection, the whites wanted no trouble with him now; in fact, they were anxious to have the power of his group with them. Thus they gave him no hassle as he went about releasing all the blacks in the cellblock; all but one, a paranoid schizophrenic named Paulina Paul, who the minister thought would be safer in his cell than roaming among the berserk convicts. Once in Cellhouse 6, where his people were headquartered, he was given a rundown on what had occurred thus far. When a Chicano contingent came to see him a few minutes later and asked him to be the spokesman for the blacks in the riot, he'd heard enough to be sure of his answer. Between the torture of Archie Martinez and the free flow of drugs, he saw the handwriting on the wall. He was an educated, religous man, and the trend of this uprising offended his sensibilities. "This isn't for us," he told them. "We don't want anything to do with it. We won't interfere with you, but we won't participate either." Reluctantly the Chicanos accepted his decision and left. But the blacks knew they'd taken a dangerous position; the Muslin leader's first plan of action was to look for a way out of the prison before the rioters decided to off them as traitors.

Back in Cellblock 4, five Chicanos were looking for an ace lieutenant, one of the most criminally insane men in the institution, a convict who'd raped his own wife with a hot curling iron. Once freed, he armed himself with a butcher knife provided by a bro and became a leading figure on the death squad that had already begun doling out retribution to chosen snitches. The dozen or so men who made up the squad—members of the Aryan Brotherhood, the Mexican Mafia, and a few unaffiliated blacks—broke up into bands of four or five and roamed the three floors of the cellblock, opening the jammed cell doors with the flames of cutting torches while they verbally gnawed on the mind of the victim trapped inside, describing in florid detail the tortures they would subject him to once the door was opened.

Up on the top tier, a large black executioner wielding a machinelike knife stood alone in front of the cell of the prison's number-one snitch. "Aha, sucker, I got you by the balls now," he announced, hacking away at the sheets that were wrapped around the bars of the door and cell. But the informer was a survivor. "The fuck you do," he answered, unshaken by the confrontation. He'd also jammed his door with the bed and armed himself with a clublike chair leg. Every time the executioner put his hand out to whack away the sheets, the snitch slammed it with the weapon. The black man saw he was getting nowhere and stopped. "I'll be back, cocksucker, with a cuttin' torch to burn you out of there, then we'll see how fuckin' tough you are."

When his tormenter was gone, the informer seized on the first opportunity to get himself out of there. A Chicano himself, he pleaded with the first homeboy to pass by his cell and got lucky. The man he chose was a newcomer and didn't recognize the snitch as anyone but an ethnic brother. He went to the office where the mechanism controlling the locking of the cells was and flipped the switch to the informant's door. Quickly the snitch scurried out and down the catwalk, bandana pulled over his face, ski cap on his head, prison-issued jacket covering the overalls with "SEG." stamped on his back, looking like the rest of the rioters rushing through the cellblock. Others were also escaping this way. "Hey, open up my cell door so I can get out and kill me some people," they'd say to the cons passing by their cells. If they weren't on the hit list or weren't recognized, their doors would be unlocked. All but twelve men in the cellblock were set free eventually; the execution squad was selective because there was an ethic to their madness, though they gave many Protection residents harrowing time to wonder whether their number was up before they were released. Even then, those lucky enough to get out of their cells had no way of knowing that the rioters were being choosy about who they killed; they fearfully dressed like the rest of the crazed cons, grabbed weapons, and made their way out of the unit either to participate in destruction in other parts of the prison or to find a hiding place. The number-one snitch who managed to escape before his black tormenter could return had the sense to know he could not take his chances mingling; he sought a hiding place. He was on the top tier of Cellblock 3 looking up at the ceiling, trying to find the fine crack that would tell him the plasterboard had been cut to provide a stash for someone's home-brew or weapons; he knew he could fit in the two-foot crawl space between the board and the real ceiling. But he was caught unaware by another Chicano who recognized him, stuck a teargas gun in his back, and marched him downstairs to the basement of Cellblock 3. Luck was with the informer, though. In the process of the journey, his captor ran into some friends and stopped to talk to them. The snitch instantly took advantage of the moment, and aided by the thick smoke that filled the corridor and hampered visibility, ran to the basement tier of the hospital. There he found a fellow informer who'd cut a hiding place in the false ceiling and was happy to share it. The two remained there for the entire riot, probably offering many thanks to their god as they listened to the agonized screams of their brother snitches whose luck had run out.

Those screams wailed through all the cellblocks on the north side. The guards held hostage there had to be having nightmare visions of the torture causing them and the specter of being the next victim. Captain Roybal, who had already been through a brutal ordeal as one of the first guards captured, suffered a mild heart attack. Whatever he'd imagined, it came nowhere near the demoniac reality that he taken over in Cellblock 4.

Some were killed the easy way, cremated to death by gasoline or paint thinner thrown into their cells along with a lit match or the flames of the torch. Others paid the hard way. One man was held down, convulsing as his executioners hammered a metal rod through his head. When they stopped, the man was dead, blood soaked his face and the hands and clothes of his killers, and the rod stuck out of the other side of his skull.

Across the way on the other side of the tier a group led by a member of the Aryan Brotherhood approached the cell of a white man who we'll call Bear. The leader recognized Bear not as a snitch but a sniveller who'd gone to the Man and asked to be locked up because he couldn't pay a gambling debt to someone in the brotherhood. Bear hadn't jammed his cell door, and now, while one of the death squad was walking to the control center to unlock it, he used the wits he'd planned to count on and begged for his life. "Please, give me a break, you know I'm a bro. I'll do anything you say," he told him. The biker thought it over for a second, then, with a malicious grin, answered, "Okay, we'll give you a chance. If you kill the nigger in the cell next to you, we'll let you live." Bear swallowed hard as his door slid open. He wasn't a killer; he'd made his deal, though, and for his own life's sake, he agreed to the initiation. The "nigger" he was to murder was Paulina Paul, the paranoid schizophrenic the Black Muslim minister had left in his cell for safety's sake.

Paulina Paul was one of the penitentiary's ten percent who'd been diagnosed as mentally ill. He'd been regarded as crazy even in childhood, and considering the name his parents cursed him with, it's no wonder: Imagine growing up as a stud in a black neighborhood with the name of a girl! Criminal insanity ran in Paulina Paul's family. His brother went berserk in a Viet Nam movie theater, fatally shooting five fellow American soldiers and wounding four others. Another brother shot a cop in Albuquerque; and his sister killed her three-year-old child.[5] Compared to their deeds, Paulina Paul's armed robbery of a hotel in Alamogordo, New Mexico, was peanuts. His actions during his trial, however, even surpassed that of his siblings. He had to be tied to his chair to keep him in the courtroom which didn't stop him from bombarding judge and jury with "loud, animal-type noises" and "religious chants."[6] Nevertheless, he was convicted as

if he were sane. He was first sent to the mental hospital
in Las Vegas, New Mexico, until they deemed him fit
to serve his sentence in Santa Fe. Even Dr. Orner
knew Paulina Paul wasn't sane enough to withstand
population. Convicts are notorious for their lack of
tolerance toward mental illness. Paulina was sent to
lockup in Cellblock 3, where he could be by himself
and loll about naked on the cold cement floor, one of
his favorite pastimes.[7]

Now Paulina Paul was to experience a death that
matched the insanity of his thirty-six years. As his cell
door was opened, Bear ran inside and plunged a
butcher knife into Paulina's stomach. It wasn't a fatal
puncture, however. Paulina staggered out onto the
tier, howling in pain and clutching the wound.

"Here, let me show you how it's done," the lead
executioner said, taking the butcher knife from Bear.
He grabbed Paulina by his hair and jerked him to the
floor. While the other four held the squirming black
man down, the biker first hacked then sawed through
his neck, muttering curses about niggers and insanity,
tenaciously severing skin, bone, and muscle until
Paulina Paul was dead and his head rolled off his body.
He had the distinction of being the only black killed in
the riot.

Meanwhile another group of executioners on the
second tier of the cellblock had just burned a cell door
off its hinges. They dragged the terrified occupant out,
tied him spread-eagle to the bars, and started beating
him with pipes and riot batons. His screams of "please
don't kill me, let me live, I want to go home . . . I want
to see my mother . . . I want to see my wife just one
more time," only brought sadistic laughter and re-
newed vigor to the beating. They didn't let up until the

man lapsed into unconsciousness. Then they untied him and threw him over the catwalk railing, watching as he landed back first on the ground floor, his legs twitching in a final throe of agonized life. At the same time, three men on the floor above had bashed an inmate's head against the wall, slipped a rope around his neck, and hung him from the railing, where his corpse dangled until a band of rioters not involved in the killings cut it down.

There were many such groups following in the wake of the executioners, ferociously slashing open stomachs, cutting off genitalia, beating on the corpses that were strewn over the catwalks. The floors were covered with clotted pools of blood, the cells with bloody drag marks, the air with the cries of men being tortured. Executioners and scavengers alike were so inundated with barbiturates they hardly saw or heard the horror they were producing. To them it was one more day in the jungle, but this day they were free to be the predators. The death dealers felt no guilt; they were acting on the strict prison ethic of payback; and the scavengers were only adding their vengeance to a deed already done. They were in their heyday, working off months and years of pent-up rage, gouging out eyes, pounding on bloated bodies. When a group of them found Paulina Paul's decapitated head, they stuck it on top of a broomstick and paraded around the prison with it in a primitive rite of victory. They had the decency to eventually return it to Paulina's body, where it remained until the riot approached its end. Then negotiators brought the corpse outside the building with the head stuck between its legs, a warning to officials of what would happen if inmates' demands were not met.

They would have struck more fear in the officials' hearts if they'd brought out the charred remains of the two men tortured to death with the pressured flames of acetyline torches. One, an informant, was held down by four of the executioners while a fifth turned the torch straight into his eyes, burning them until the back of his head exploded from the pressure and heat. Those who found his body later could still see the terror on what was left of his face. This murder was seen by a prison secretary watching through binoculars from the perimeter fence outside the penitentiary. "I heard some whistling and I looked over toward the cells and they just had a torch and were burning somebody's head," she told newspeople afterwards. "He was screaming. I couldn't believe it. It was like a nightmare."

The worst nightmare in the cellblock, however, was the execution of thirty-four-year-old James Perrin. The death squad saved him for last. Perrin was serving a life sentence for raping and murdering two little girls and their mother. In every prison in the nation, baby rapers ("short eyes") are despised, the one criminal in the jungle worse than all the others, someone even the most deranged convict can look down on. Everyone, after all, especially when insecure and oppressed, needs someone they can feel better than. Jimmy Perrin had barricaded himself in his cell, thanks to the advice of his next-door neighbor, who'd been like a brother to him since moving to the adjacent cell a year before. Perrin's friend had instructed him in the ways and means of protecting himself, knowing he'd be a sure target for death. By the time the rioters broke into the unit, Perrin's fear had thrown him into shock. When one of the executioners stood in front of his cell soon after their entry, taunting him with threats of death and mutilation, Perrin stood mute and glassy-eyed behind his bed, leaning his full three hundred pounds against it to keep the legs jamming the door. All the torches were in use at the time, so the executioner had to put off his plans for the baby raper. "I'll be back to cut you out of there later, man," he promised, and went on his way. When Perrin's friend was freed by other residents of the cellblock, he tried to convince him to take the barricade down and come out with him. But James had slipped into catatonia. All he could do was stand in back of the upraised bed, pushing it rhythmically as if he were a dog humping a table leg, saying nothing, looking like his mind had gone. That was the last his friend saw of him. When he came back to Cellblock 4 thirty minutes later to try and talk James out of the cell again, he didn't even both going inside. He heard Perrin's screams and knew it was too late.

James Perrin wasn't proud of the crime he'd committed, as he explained in a letter to a woman whose friendship he tried to cultivate four months before he died. Like most criminals, his undoing was a lack of love and education, deficiencies that caused intense emotional instability when triggered by the normal heartbreaks of living.

> First let me say that you might of heard of me. I was known as one of the Chaparrel killers. I was born in Deming, New Mexico, and then when I was twenty-two moved to El Paso, Texas, with my wife. We got a divorce in 1977 and I started going to pieces. On the street I push eighteen wheels around the countryside for a living. Yes, I make good money. And that's what causes my trouble in my marriage. I work too hard for a good

living for them and she didn't care for that or me. Now here I am, I was running from state to state picking up work here and there and just living in my truck, until I came back to El Paso to see my sister. And now this thing happens to me. Now I look back and see myself, and the truth is so ugly to take. You see, I am thirty-three years old and I have nobody to really call a friend. I would like to write and carry on a correspondence with somebody and especially of the opposite sex. I just want to be liked and loved by someone who cares.

There would be no caring for Jimmy Perrin in this life. After blowtorching his door open, four executioners, including the one who'd originally taunted him, dragged James out of his cell, tied him spread-eagle to the bars, and cooked him slowly with the roaring flame of the acetyline torch, melting his three hundred pounds of flesh to bone. They worked on him for half an hour, first burning his genitals, then his face, moving the torch up and down his body, bringing him around with smelling salts when he drifted into the comfort of unconsciousness until nothing could bring him back anymore. Maybe this was enough penance to save Jimmy Perrin from any future hells.

VIII

When I came in, the Penitentiary of New Mexico was only six years old. It had been built because the situation at the old prison had become so explosive the legislature could no longer avoid the issue. Brick and mortar do not a change make, however. The same conditions that forced the closing of the old facility continued. All the state had bought itself was a newer, larger animal house.

The situation had been intolerable for five years before the legislature even decided to investigate the old institution, no less make any changes. It's the same old problem that has existed since the beginning of penal institutions: The public doesn't want to know about them; they don't want to think about what makes a human being become a so-called criminal any more than they want to know how he's treated once he's been arrested. They're content to hide him away in a remote fortress: out of sight, out of mind. But America is finding out that this old adage no longer holds true when it comes to the treatment of its criminal element. People are discovering that it's the penitentiaries themselves that are keeping the crime rate up. Most convicts are going to be back on the streets after they've served their sentences, and they're going to be filled with the hate and rage prison life incites. The fact is, U.S. prisons are not only hate factories, they're crime factories. But as long as John Q. Public refuses to look the problem in the eye, neither will the senators and representatives who could initiate change. Only when inmates take the matter into their own hands and cause a disturbance big enough to draw the public's attention to them do legislators act. Consequently, to the mind of a convict, riots are a legitimate means of communication.

In December 1948 the residents of the Penitentiary of New Mexico rioted in protest over the bad food and the steward in charge of cooking it. Six months later a fight between two prisoners stirred other inmates into expressing their frustrations in a violent disturbance in the prison yard. In November 1950 another riot erupted over a "feud between prisoners and guard,"[2] as the legislative committee report gently termed it; in this a number of guards were injured. There was an unsuccessful escape attempt in June 1952 that caused a guard to be killed and the warden to resign. Six months hence there was another escape attempt, with the escapees forcing open a vault and confiscating the guns stored inside it. These convicts were subdued before the weapons could be used or they could get away. But tensions in the prison did not ease up. The next month there was a fight between rival gangs that left one inmate stabbed to death and several others wounded. Even after these four years of constant violent eruptions, New Mexico's legislature didn't take immediate action. It took yet another uprising by inmates to make the public insist that their government representatives do something about the penitentiary. And wait for their constituency to insist is what every politician does in the matter of prisons and crime, not a popular subject or one to get caught on the wrong side of if one desires a long political career. As former Governor Jerry Apodaca summed it up in explaining why his efforts to reform the penitentiary failed, "Who cares about the penitentiary? Inmates? Well, how many are there, twelve hundred, maybe thirteen hundred at the highest? They can't even vote; they're a very small constituency. Sure, they have families, they have friends, but sometimes the local pressures from society are much greater."[3]

In 1953, the New Mexico Legislature at last assigned a committee to investigate the causes of violence in the state's prison. The expert they brought in to head this inquiry was Douglas C. Rigg, former assistant warden at San Quentin. Rigg's report blamed the institution's problems on factors that have existed in prisons since their inception and continue to exist in the "enlightened" 1980's: "an inadequate system of classifying inmates for placement and security . . . idleness, lack of education and recreation, insufficient medical services, untrained and underpaid guards, and little dissemination of information to the press and public."[4] Rigg told the legislative committee that "the incidents [of violence] are actually symptoms and not causes of bad conditions. The conditions outlined in my report took years to develop. I believe my recommendations will help improve them. *In the last analysis, the prison conditions are the responsibility of the legislature, which expresses the will of the people.*"[5] The will of New Mexico's people was to apply brick and mortar to the situation, plus a dollop of good intentions with which to pave the road to the future.

New Mexico's new penitentiary opened on April 20, 1956, with the usual ribbon-cutting ceremony and public relations hype calling it a model of humane corrections. To illustrate this, the state handed out a press release listing "fifty brief facts and figures about the institution,"[6] citing the million gallons of water the pumps could move each day, the 132,000 bags of cement used to construct the facility, and the $24,000 spent on the gas chamber. The release ended with a brief statement of political rhetoric: "Walls and bars make a prison, but they don't change men for the better. Our objective, through group and individual training, is to try to discharge these men to the free community as law-abiding, responsible citizens who can and will support themselves and their dependents."[7] But by 1958, two years after the prison opened, Warden H. R. Swenson was reporting to the legislature that "the major problem facing the penitentiary now is prisoner idleness. If all the jobs were counted up, there would be work for about three hundred men . . . although New Mexico has one of the finest penal institutions in the country, it could be destroyed in a year if the men are not kept occupied."[8] As well and as usual, there was the problem of prison personnel. "Of greatest importance . . . is the selection, training, and proper utilization of personnel," Warden Swenson said. "The old concept of the officer who is only a guard is giving way to the recognition that he is actually a supervisor and as such has responsibilities requiring qualifications, training, and compensation beyond those required for purely security work."[9] Again, however, the politicians didn't listen well enough. The legislature was willing to provide money for literally concrete changes but not for people, neither in terms of rehabilitation programs nor in raises for corrections officers.

In 1956 a guard's starting salary was $265 a month; a stenographer in a secretarial pool was making as much. This was nowhere near enough money to attract a man with intelligence, sensitivity, or education to the dangerous field of overseeing caged criminals. Studies bear this out. They show that only one out of two guards in the nation's prisons is even a high school graduate, and only one out of three has been to college; not graduated, either, just attended. A Rhode Island college professor named Allan Berman did a survey of a hundred applicants for jobs in that state's prisons and found that most of them showed "emotional shallowness, alienation from social customs, and relative inability to profit from social sanctions."[10] The University of Rhode Island's psychology department also tested correctional officer applicants against prison inmates to see the "violence potential" of each. The tests showed the two groups were almost identical, with the guards coming out more violent than the inmates! "The officer group actually has the potential for even more unexplained lashing out than does the inmate group . . . the officer candidates are as likely as the inmates to engage in assaultive behavior."[11] In congressional hearings, too, evidence has piled up to prove that the occupation of correctional officer "appeals to those who like to wield power over the powerless and to persons of sadistic bent."[12] For the ridiculous wages paid—even in 1980 the starting salary for a guard at the Penitentiary of New Mexico was a lowly $765 a month—it's understandable that the only reason a man would take the job would be out of desperation or hate.

Hate is just a short jump away from the judgmental, holier-than-thou attitude that formed the concept of the American penitentiary. In 1787 Philadelphian Dr. Benjamin Rush walked into good old Ben Franklin's home and proposed that the "right way to treat offenders was to make them repent their crimes . . . offenders should be locked alone in cells day and night, so that in such awful solitude they would have nothing to do but to ponder their acts, repent, and reform."[13] From Dr. Rush's idea evolved the "Auburn system," the model for the penitentiary of today. That system added a sadistic twist to Dr. Rush's original notion. Elam Lynds, the first warden of Sing Sing, which was built in 1825, summed up the philosophy that has guided the thinking of corrections officials in this country for the past 150 years: "Reformation of the criminal could not possibly be effected until the spirit of the criminal was broken."[14] This has not proven to be the case. If there's been any reformation at all from the prison experience it's been to turn petty thieves into killers and lifetime residents of the nation's maximum security facilities, all under the banner of rehabilitation and the actuality of punishment. Ask any warden or guard or prison administrator what he thinks about the possibilities of rehabilitation or what his true opinion of a convict is. If you catch him in a rare moment of honesty, he'll tell you that he sees the inmate as something less than human and punishment as the only thing that works to keep him in line.

The law, too, upholds this view. When a person is convicted of committing a felony, he forfeits all individual rights; he is in a state of civil death. "He has, as a consequence of his crime, not only forfeited his liberty, but all his personal rights except those which the law in its humanity accords to him. He is for the time being the slave of the state."[15] This is the courts' interpretation of the Thirteenth Amendment as it applies to law breakers: "Neither slavery nor involuntary servitude, *except as a punishment for crime whereof the party shall have been duly convicted,* shall exist within the United States." Because the law of the land holds that a convict is in this state of civil death, the courts likewise uphold the autonomy of the prison administrators in running the country's penal institutions. They have ruled that "courts are without power to supervise prison administration or to interfere with the ordinary prison rules or regulations."[16] Once the gates of the animal farm close around a person convicted of committing a crime, he answers only to the law of the poorly paid, emotionally shallow, alienated, potentially violent, sadistic men who, studies have shown, flock to the fields of corrections.

Maybe the old way of treating criminals before the penitentiary system was instituted was more humane than prison life; certainly it more honestly reflected the attitude of society toward those who broke its laws. If you committed a crime in the early days of America, you knew you were going to feel the revenge of the citizenry. You'd be beheaded or hanged, flogged, stretched on the rack, tortured, blinded, tarred and feathered, ridden out of town on a rail, or spread-eagled in the stocks for all to stare at. No one pretended they were trying to reform you; they were just giving you your due reward for acting in violation of the community's codes. And it was an instant reward. If your crime didn't warrant beheading or hanging, you had an opportunity to resume your life with the immediate scar of that punishment to remind you of the folly of your old ways. Today, the psychological scar of years of mental and physical torture wipes out any thought of conforming to the society that inflicted it. In fact, the convict learns to behave as brutally as those who uphold the law of the land within the prison. I'm certainly not suggesting we go back to the rack or the stocks; I'm just saying that we still haven't found a way of dealing with the so-called criminal element in our culture.

This opens the other side of the question: Who are we building our prisons for? People have been trying to figure out what makes a criminal for at least the past two hundred years. Many theories have been expounded, but all have been rubbed out by each generation's new ideas on the subject. It used to be thought that the devil was to blame. In the nineteenth century the English accused criminals of "being prompted and instigated by the Devil."[17] In 1862 the North Carolina Supreme Court followed its ancestors' train of thought by declaring: "To know the right and still the wrong pursue proceeds from a perverse will brought about by the seductions of the Evil One."[18] Toward the end of the nineteenth century Italian criminologist Cesare Lombroso took the blame away from the devil and gave it to God. Criminals are born that way, he said, "not a variation from the norm, but practically a special species, a subspecies, having distinct physical and mental characteristics."[19] In the 1930s came another theory, from a German this time. His studies showed that certain physical types were more prone to crime than others: Men who were stout and squat and had large abdomens were usually the occasional offenders, while slender men with slight muscular builds were most often habitual criminals. The 1940s expanded on this with the gland analysis that named the criminals of the world mesomorphs." In physical type the mesomorph was the reverse of the previous decade's description. Instead of short and fat, the criminal was now thought to be muscular, bearlike, assertive, noisy, and aggressive. During all these speculations on the physique of the criminal, the doctors who were engaged in the budding new field of psychology and psychiatry were putting in their two cents worth. In 1920 a Princeton psychologist, Dr. Henry Goddard, thought that criminals were people of low mentality, but by 1959 that theory was soundly disproven. "Studies of prison populations made by clinical psychologists demonstrate that those behind bars compare favorably with the general population in intelligence. Since we seldom arrest and convict criminals except the poor, inept, and friendless, we can know very little of the intelligence of the bulk of the criminal world. It is quite possible that it is, by and large, superior."[20] Indeed, it is currently held that the criminal mind and the creative mind are but two sides of the same potential, the one being undeveloped, uneducated, and frustrated.

More than just the "poor, inept and friendless" have criminal minds. In the late 1940s, 1700 anonymous New Yorkers, all in the upper-income bracket and who'd never been arrested, answered questions about their criminal activities. It turned out that 91 percent of them—64 percent of the men and 27 percent of the women—had committed a felony for which they could have been sent to the state pen had they been caught and convicted.[21] Poverty, it was clear even to theorizers in 1870, was the major factor in the making of a criminal. In those days the prisons were filled with Irish and Italian immigrants, the young, the poor, the native Americans. Today they're filled with the new immigrants the country takes in with open arms that close the minute the boat lands; our own slum dwellers, the blacks, Chicanos, and poor whites disenfranchised by society; as well as the young counter-culture drug users. Why is it the poor are more prone to end up in jail, while the more affluent middle class who are committing as many felonies aren't? It's not just a matter of lack of money for legal fees, because the middle-class whites aren't even apprehended for their crimes. It's been demonstrated so much in our society of late that it's almost redundant to say it, but the police instantly react to blacks and other ethnic minorities as if they were criminals. In a book called *The Myth of the Criminal Type,* the author, Professor Theodore Sarbin, says,

> The belief that some classes of persons were "dangerous" guided the search for suspects. . . . Laws are broken by many citizens for many rea-

sons: Those suspects who fit the concurrent social type of the criminal are most likely to become objects of police suspicion. . . . To account for the disproportionate number of lower-class and black prisoners, I propose that the agents of law enforcement and justice engage in decision-making against a backcloth of belief that people can be readily classified into two types, criminal and non-criminal.[22]

The President's crime commission made the same observations in 1967:

A policeman in attempting to solve crimes must employ, in the absence of concrete evidence, circumstantial indicators to link specific crimes with specific people. Thus policemen may stop Negro and Mexican youths in white neighborhoods, may suspect juveniles who act in what the policemen consider an impudent or overly casual manner, and may be influenced by such factors as unusual hair styles or clothes uncommon to the wearer's group or area . . . those who act frightened, penitent, and respectful are more likely to be released, while those who assert their autonomy and act indifferent or resistant run a substantially greater risk of being frisked, interrogated, or even taken into custody.[23]

For all this, we still haven't determined the root cause of the making of a criminal. The thread that runs throughout every finding, though, is poverty: financial poverty, opportunity poverty, educational poverty, love poverty, and finally, self-worth poverty. All these begin in childhood. With the majority of criminals who get caught, there is a pattern of one kind of neglect or another in their early family life. My own beginnings are an example. Though I have known convicts who've suffered far more, the result is still the same: a self-hatred that cannot be tolerated, that must be projected onto the world at large bacause the pain is too great to face; for most people, but especially for men in this society, anger and rebellion are the response to the wounds of early conditioning.

I never really knew my mother or father, particularly my father. He was an alcoholic and died of cirrhosis of the liver after I started my criminal endeavors. When I was three years old, my parents divorced and my mother put me in a foster home. I don't know whether she didn't want me or couldn't take care of me; I never gave it much thought, so it didn't bother me. In other words, I buried my feelings. The family I was farmed out to treated me well enough. They were a German couple who had grandchildren my age. They were very strict but fortunately not mean. There were no beatings but no affection, either. My foster father didn't provide much of a male figure for me to learn from. He worked nights as a baker, came home as I was going to school, said hello, and that was the last I'd see of him until the next morning. My childhood was lifeless; no emotions of either love or hate within myself or from others. I deadened them as I saw everyone around me deaden theirs. I spent fifteen years of empty time waiting to grow up and be on my own. At fifteen, I joined the army with a fake ID. When I came out at eighteen with an honorable discharge and few hundred dollars in my pocket, I felt like the world owed me a living. I had no desire to work. Finding a job wouldn't have been easy, anyway. I didn't have a high school diploma—I'd left school after finishing the ninth grade; I had a complex about the way I expressed myself, knowing I sounded ignorant, and I didn't really have a trade, at least not one I wanted to work out. I'd done some welding and plumbing in the army, but I'd had enought of it. I wanted to do something I hadn't done before; I wanted to be out in the world and decided hitchhiking around the country would satisfy my itch for freedom. I did it until one morning when I woke up in a Las Vegas motel room with seventy-five cents in my pocket, feeling broke and desperate with nowhere and no one to turn to for help. I reasoned that with only seventy-five cents to my name, the need for money seemed more immediate than the need to find a job, which would take days; a simple robbery seemed the best alternative. Fate presented me with the opportunity not five minutes later. As I walked into the motel lobby to spend fifty of my seventy-five cents on a pack of smokes to help me scheme a plan, I saw the manager counting out the money from the night's receipts. I thought, This is as good a time as any. I took the pocketknife I carried out of my pocket, walked up behind him, put the knife to his back, and told him it was a stickup. He handed me the money without any fuss and got down on the floor until I left, as I told him to. I walked out and took the first bus out of town. I scored eight hundred dollars, more than I could legitimately earn in six weeks. It seemed so easy I kept on pulling bigger and bigger robberies, rationalizing that I'd continue stealing only until I figured out what I really wanted to do in life. Life doesn't work that way, though; three and a half years after I started my criminal career, I got busted. Those first nine years in the penitentiary didn't do anything to change my mind about crime. When I was finally paroled after being

one of the hardcore cons, it took only fourteen months
for me to sink into the despair that led me to robbing so
many years before. It was Christmas, I'd lost my job
and my girlfriend and was down to my last thirty dollars. I felt like I had nothing to lose even if I did go
back to Sante Fe, which I did. It was as if life were
taking me by the scruff of the neck and saying, "Look,
you sorry sucker, you're going to learn some lessons
whether you like it or not." And learn I did in the next
five years, but not because I had any help from either
prison officials or inmates. If it takes fourteen years for
a penitentiary to reform a man's way of thinking,
something's got to be wrong with the system.

One of the major things wrong with it is the absence
of normal sexual relations. It's perverse to lock up
men in their sexual prime and not provide a normal
outlet for their erotic desires. We're dealing with pas-
sionate, needing, angry people here, not saints and
ascetics ready to take up celibacy. Further, the soft-
ness of a female would do a lot to calm down the furies
that rage inside an inmate. Not only do prison authorities forbid sexual relations between men and
women, they have tight restrictions on how much a
man can simply *kiss* his own wife or girlfriend during
visits. But the appetites will be satisfied, even if reluctantly. It took me five years to succumb to the ad-
vances of a jailhouse queen. During the years preceeding I relied on my right hand and my fertile fantasies,
like so many inmates do. But there's no privacy in
prison; masturbation, like sex, has to be public or
snuck in corners of darkness. I didn't like myself being
with a man sexually, so I soon stopped and returned to
my solitary pleasures. Many did like being with men,
however—many who were not queens on the street
but who worked out thier violent streaks along with

their orgasms. Rape was the going mode of sexual fulfillment in the prison population:

> Prison rape contributes heavily to the ethic of force that dominates every prison. The patterns of prison sex, in fact, raise sharply the question whether what a former prison medical officer has called "forced segregation of dangerous individuals within a small perimeter" makes any sense at all. These sex patterns are one more assurance that most inmates will leave prison more antisocial than they were when they entered.[24]

I was initiated into the ritual of prison rape on my first night in population. Some noises near my bunk woke me. When I opened my eyes, I saw three black inmates standing over the dude in the bed next to mine. We'd both just come out of Quarrantine, and like me, he was young and white. His eyes were wide with fear. One of the blacks held a large knife over his head. "Roll over, boy," he said. The kid had no choice. I'll never forget the look on his face as he turned over onto his stomach. He was naked except for the sheet that covered him. The black with the knife pulled it down and mounted him, thrusting his huge cock into the poor guy's asshole with no pity and no grease to ease the pain. They had to cover his mouth to stifle his scream. When the first one was finished, the other two took their turns. By then the kid's muffled cries had turned into humiliated whimpering. When all three had finished, they returned to their beds at the other end of the dormitory. I laid there without moving, just listening to the kid's quiet crying. I stayed awake the rest of the night. It was then I swore I'd become such a hardcore con that no one would ever come near me like that.

IX

A prison film after Fellini. Fade in . . . enter the Archbishop. The Archbishop of Santa Fe . . . is given a tour of the prison by abject officialdom. When he emerges, he is surrounded by his parishioners, overwhelmed, almost, by shouted questions. What has become of my husband? My son? You will be pleased to know, he tells them, that . . . amid all the rubble, smashed cellblocks, burned gymnasium, the chapel had been spared. This is a powerful indication, he tells them, of the love of God, the faith in Jesus, that still fills the hearts of the prisoners. But what of my husband? My son? The archbishop silences their questions, spreads his hands. Let us pray. The archbishop turns away from the crowd. Behind are the questions he cannot answer. Inside is the carnage he dared not be first to reveal. Water. Fire. Powdered toilets. Charred relations. The stabbed, the hanged, the cleaved—dead in their own excrement . . . The parishioners remain by the highway, where they have stood for many hours— men, women, children . . . there is no place to sit *but the rocky ground; there is no place to relieve oneself. Of anything. But such things are temporal; they are not of the spirit. People may be dead inside, their screams still hanging on the walls, but God is alive and well in the gleaming chapel. The archbishop drives back to town. The camera follows him. Sooner or later it will catch him washing his hands.*

—ROBERT MAYER[1]

Saturday, February 2, 1980. The massacre of the men in Cellblock 4 went on until mid-morning. All over the penitentiary the screams of the tortured victims could be heard, with interspersed radio transmissions announcing, "We just killed five more down here. . . . " Only the strongest stomachs were able to stand the smell of burning flesh that permeated the air, especially in the units on the north side where I was. I saw a lot of men bend over and puke their guts out to get the disgusting combination of sound, odor, and mental pictures out of their systems. It wasn't until 10:30 or 11:00, three and a half to four hours after the death squad had entered the protection unit that the screaming stopped, though the sickening fatty stench never left the atmosphere.

I was about to go down to the hospital to find some aspirin when an old friend of mine walked into the old men's dormitory and asked if we had any coffee. I gave him some and he and I sat down and started rapping. He looked like he'd just come out of a Viet Nam raid, his face smeared with black soot and blood, his hair a matted mess, his prison fatigues covered with splotches of dried, brown blood. Then I spotted a screwdriver sticking out of his back pocket.

"Hey, that screwdriver in your pocket, there," I said, "it looks like it's got some blood on it."

"Yeah, I got me a few down in 4," he bragged.

"Well, what happened? Run it down."

And he did, describing in full detail the killings he'd seen his buddies participate in, plus his own deeds: He'd stabbed three men in the chest with his screwdriver, bashed in another's head, and burned another alive by throwing gasoline into his jammed cell.

While he was talking, I started thinking. I'd come a long way in fourteen years. Even six years ago I might have given some thought to paying back a snitch or a welcher. Ten years ago I gave it more than a thought; I actually shafted a dude who'd run off with our dope money. Fortunately, though I didn't think so at the time, he didn't die. As I listened to this man go on about the murders he'd seen in Cellblock 4, I knew that even then I wouldn't have participated in what he was describing; a sickness had taken these men over, and I thanked God I hadn't been afflicted by it, this time or any time. Still, I had to keep up my hardcore front with my old friend; I'd known him a long time in the joint, but if he'd gone as overboard as he was saying, who knew when he'd snap on me. I couldn't tell if he was slurring his words because of drugs or fatigue, but in either case, he'd be hypersensitive, especially after using me as a confessional.

"Man, I would've been down there with you," I told him, "but I got my parole comin' up in two months."

"I can dig it, bro, Just keep your eyes open; anyone thinks you been sittin' on your ass up here and hiding out's liable to kill you if they catch you by yourself.

We've finished with what we set out to do in 4, but there's a lot of other guys out there in population gettin' knocked off right now. Just make sure you cover your back if you do step out into it."

I finished my coffee, thanked him for the advice, and got away from him as fast as I could. I gathered several friends from the dorm, and together, with extreme caution, we embarked into the madness. First we hit the hospital, not for anything more exotic than aspirin, which I found. Then we made our way down to the kitchen to try and get some food. My headache was not only from revulsion but from hunger; we hadn't eaten anything since six o'clock the night before. Getting through to the kitchen was no easy task. The corridor was filled with doped rioters shouting and hollering at each other, stampeding back and forth in the smokey haze. We found very little food; the kitchen had been totally trashed and raided. Some cans of tomatoes had been left and we were happy to have them, though they were one of our least favorite foods when the prison served them. On our way back we stopped to take a look at Cellblock 4. I had a friend there and wanted to find out what had happened to him. I didn't locate him because I got lost in the bodies and blood that were strewn all over the place; corpses hanging from the railing, sticking out between the bars of a cell. I saw one man hanging on a door with a rod through his skull, another with his genitals laying next to him. Between these visions and the odor of shit and burned flesh that filled my nostrils, I felt like running out, but I forced myself to go through the tier and see for myself the devastation.

There is no way I can transmit the full horror of that scene any more than there's any way I can erase it from my mind's eye. It's better for those whose lives did not lead them to witness it that it can't be described in all it's bloody detail. My only point in recounting the savagery of this riot is to etch the picture of prison life as it really is into the public mind so indelibly that people can never erase from their consciousness the product of inhumane treatment. Think of it: Though my screwdriver-wielding executioner friend is a lifer, he's eligible for parole after he's served ten or fifteen years of his sentence. He'll be out on the streets again after all he's learned about being the most violent dude on the block in the penitentiary, sitting next to you on a bus, maybe. If you look at him wrong and he's feeling depressed or if he's broke and you look flush, what has your tax money taught him during his ten years in prison in terms of dealing with life? It's taught him to hate, to steal, to fight, to kill, and he's more than likely to use one or all of those talents on you.

Others learn how to rape their own sex, how to take their most sublime ecstasy in an act of violent sodomy. James Foley was a nineteen-year old peach-fuzzed kid from Albuquerque who'd just come into the penitentiary in December 1979 to do a life sentence for the first-degree murder of the manager of a Circle K store he was robbing. Foley was big, six-foot-four, two hundred pounds, and like most kids when they first enter the joint, he tried to cover his youth and his fear by acting tough. For James Foley, it didn't work. The first week he was in population he was beaten by a group from the Chicano clique. The administration locked him up in Protection for a few weeks, then made the mistake of putting him back in population a week or so before the riot. It didn't matter why he'd gone to Protection; the very fact that he'd wound up there made him a punk in a convict's eyes. In the midst of the riot on Saturday afternoon, that same group of Chicanos found him again, sitting on his bunk in Dormitory A-1, trying to stay out of everyone's way. As he saw the eight rioters approach his bed wielding pipes and bats, he became terrified and started crying, begging them not to bother him. But they answered by telling him to take off his clothes. He did, mistakenly thinking obedience would save him. When he was naked, they told him to lay down on his side and clasp his hands under his knees. Tying his wrists together so that he was bound in this fetal position, they turned him over onto his stomach, and each of the eight barbiturated men took their turn sodomizing him, while others whacked him severely with their pipes and bats. When they'd all had their sexual satisfaction, they pushed him off the bed and continued the beating, kicking him in the head and kidneys until he was unconscious. Later it would be discovered that he was more than unconscious. They had kicked James Foley to death.

Now the band of rapists, whose murder had been increased by other rioters, turned their attention on the residents of the dormitory. They had watched Foley's rape in fear for their own safety. A-1 was a unit where the younger inmates in the prison were housed. They had thought that by staying out of the way they would be safe and had not armed themselves. Each was tied in the same fetal position as Foley, each had a pillowcase placed over his head, and each was sodomized more than ten times. Whenever they'd made a move or a sound, a pipe or fist would hit them over the head. They'd been dimly aware of the sounds of moaning going on around them, but not until their rapists had gone on to greener pastures and the first of them untied and unhooded himself was it clear to them that the dormitory had been turned into a battlefield brothel that would have shocked the father of sadism himself. After the riot was over, one of these rape victims talked to a reporter. He was telling his story, he said, because he wanted to let America know that inmates get raped by other inmates all the time in every prison in the country. He wanted to tell it "so the public will be enlightened."[2]

While the rapists stalked the prison for more perverse ecstasy, other rioters wandered through the hallways and dormitories looking for vengeance on old enemies. In prison it takes only small incidents to make a man form a vendetta against a fellow convict, and under the influence of drugs and freed anger these grudges seemed worth killing for. Not all the payback dished out was fatal, and relatively few took part in these random revenge murders. In all, only twenty-five, including the dozen or so Cellblock 4 executioners, participated in the killings; but they ended more than thirty lives. In the light of the sober days to come, these attacks seemed senseless even to many of the perpetrators. One inmate was killed because he'd gone out with his murderer's girlfriend ten years before. Another had his eye gouged out; yet another had one testical cut off, thanks to the bad aim of his mutilator. Both lived to remember the moment and carry the scars. An inmate carefully winding his way down the main corridor to the safety of Dormitory E-2—the only unit in the entire building that was left intact, where men who wanted to mind their own business could just sit around, drink coffee, and play cards—bumped into someone accidently because the smoke was so thick he couldn't see. The next thing he knew was the heavy, cold feel of steel rods pounding on his head. Fortunately, he saw a meat cleaver coming at him in time to ward it off with his arm. The cleaver caught him on the wrist and cut clear through to the bone. The gashes on his head and arm bled profusely into the many towels a self-styled inmate paramedic kept wrapped around them until he could get medical attention and stitches hours later.

It got so frenetic that these wandering gangs weren't particular about who they attacked. If a man was walking alone, the gangs, in their convoluted thinking, would consider his very vulnerability a worthy reason to beat him and teach him a lesson about the follies of weakness. Lust for "sniff" was also a reason to kill. Two men had just gotten a jar of shoe glue from the shoe shop in the basement and were walking upstairs with it when a group of five Chicanos standing at the top of the steps saw them and demanded they turn over the precious solvent to them. The two refused and the larger group beat it and their lives away from them. There was some instant karma, too: One of the rape squad got his throat cut a few hours after he'd satiated himself in Dormitory A-1. He lived but spent a lot of hours bleeding and wondering if he would.

The majority of rioters who were not involved in these surges of rage upon their fellow convicts turned their energy to tearing apart the prison itself, setting fires everywhere, breaking everything they could get their hands on. Some found save havens, like Dormitory E-2, while others merely took their chances staggering around the hallways in a blind euphoria that hopefully made tolerable the beatings they inevitably suffered. The smarter inmates looked for a way out of the institution. They knew they were taking a chance going outside, for no officials had said, "If you want to come out, do it, we won't shoot." They had no idea what was waiting for them out there, but they knew it couldn't be any worse than the chaos closing in on them inside. About twenty men who'd escaped from Cellblock 4 had the wits to grab one of the acetyline torches on their way out and head straight for the empty Cellblock 5 across the hall. They used the torch to cut a hole in a metal door on the east end of the unit and made a hasty retreat, surrendering at the front gate in the yard. When the rioters realized what had happened, they stationed a group to guard the opening and prevent anyone else from leaving. They got there in time to stop the Black Muslim leader and thirty of his men from going through it. The Muslims weren't going to be stopped, however. They found out about the escape of the E-1 residents earlier and headed over to the south side dormitory. There, too, rioters stood guard, but this time the Muslim leader was determined. "Move aside," he announced, "we're movin' out."

"The hell you are," the rioter answered with uplifted bat.

The Muslim leader was fast and knocked his opponent to the ground with the billy club he was carrying. A few of his group took care of the rest of the guarding inmates and the opening was cleared. The blacks went through the hole one by one, with the leader out first announcing to officials that he and his gorup were surrendering. Nothing was going unavenged this day, though. The rioters stabbed the last two blacks to climb out, only wounding them, however, and not hindering their escape.

At 1:30 in the afternoon, twenty minutes after the

Muslims surrendered, another twenty inmates found
their way out. Throughout the rest of the day, men
were breaking out of the penitentiary in groups and
alone through any opening they could find, often
fighting the rioters who blocked their way. Many of
those escaping were injured, cut, and beaten either by
the inside rampage or while trying to leave. Timing
was with these wounded. Two National Guard medical
support teams, the 744 Medical Detachment and the
717th Medivac Helicopter Unit, had arrived at the
front gate just before 1:00. The helicopters quickly
transported the more seriously injured to St. Vincent's
Hospital in Santa Fe. As that hospital became overcrowded, they transferred the more stabilized patients
to Albuquerque facilities. As more inmates surrendered, more tents set up by the medical support teams
became filled with cases of bone fractures, amputa-
tions, and deep shock. Soon drug overdoses became
the number-one malady these teams were treating. Inmates coming out of the prison would carry wounded
and OD'd, unconscious rioters out into the yard up to
the front gate, where the medics, stationed behind the
fence, could get them once the gate was opened. Some
of the convicts doing the carrying did so just as an
excuse to get out, but a few stayed with the rioters,
functioning as paramedics inside the prison, treating
the wounded, hostages included, and repeatedly manning stretchers to get the seriously hurt to safety and
medical care.

The gatehouse at Tower 1 in front of the penitentiary
had become not only the administration command post
but a makeshift interrogation center where unwounded
inmates, and later released hostages who were physically able, were debriefed. The surrendering convicts
were told to walk up to the front gate ten at a time with

their hands on top of their heads. The gate would be opened, they'd be let into the ten-foot moat of land between the two perimeter fences, and told to line up with their hands on the fence while corrections officers, and any other officials handy in the confusion, frisked them. Razor blades, homemade shanks, scissors, and pockets full of pills were found. All weapons were tagged and placed in a large box that reporters and officials wandering into the gatehouse would sift through curiously throughout the riot and for days afterward. When frisking was over, the prisoners would be handcuffed with plastic wire and taken into the gatehouse for questioning. Anyone whose weapon had telltale traces of blood on it was handed over to police for special interrogation elsewhere. After the debriefing, some of the men were sent to the warm walls of the Annex, where the women inmates were usually housed, but when that unit was filled there was nowhere for them but the ten-foot-wide moat of fenced-in land that surrounded the smoldering penitentiary. These early debriefings didn't net officials much information about the hostages, but they did give them their first verification that killing was taking place inside. That it was being done at the hands of specific groups had been hinted at in an earlier radio transmission from an inmate. "There are a couple of lunatics running around that just want to get into violence," he said. "It has been creating some problems."[3] Dr. Marc Orner, one of the group conducting the questioning, had gotten enough information from the twenty men who'd broken out of Cellblock 4 to be able to identify "fifteen to twenty" inmates as those doing the murdering, and to compile a list of ten "death squad" members.

There were hostages being released, but they were

not in a condition to be questioned. The first was Officer Elton "Bigfoot" Curry. As the Cellblock 4 slaughter was beginning at sunrise, Curry's beaten, stabbed, naked body was brought out the main entrance on a mattress. The rioters had doubts that he'd live, and they didn't want him dying in their hands. They knew their ex-warden, Felix Rodriguez, would be true to his word and storm the building if one of his guards died. Thanks to radio conversations with Captain Roybal and other officers being kept in the north wing, prison officials were assured that at least some of the remaining ten hostages were alive. The rioters allowed Deputy Warden Montoya to speak with these guards so their demand that the penitentiary not be rushed could be felt. "At this moment our lives are in your hands," Officer Larry Mendoza told Montoya. "What else can I say?" Montoya spent considerable time throughout the morning promising them that their safety was his main concern, that officials would take no actions that would jeopardize it. At 8:20 A.M., Officer Mike Hernandez was carried out and handed over to medics after an hour of haggling beween the two sides of negotiators. All morning there were radio reports and snatches of conversations from inside the prison to the effect that Lieutenant Jose Anaya was in need of medical attention. An inmate called Doc who was working as a paramedic was overheard talking to another inmate on the radio: "I'm over here checking this Lieutenant Anaya," he said. "I think Anaya's got a concussion, and I think he's got a busted rib, and I know that he's got a heart condition and he needs to be moved; he needs to be taken out of here."[4] The rioters grabbed this opportunity to make a trade, offering Anaya in return for Montoya himself, or at least a medical doctor. The deputy warden refused the deal but offered them the carrot they most wanted, a meeting with the news media in return for Anaya. No agreement was struck, and the lieutenant was left to the ministering of the paramedic.

Because so many people were using the radios and confusing the transmissions, riot negotiators requested and got a field telephone for one-to-one communication with outside officials. The first person they called was the Governor. They'd not been able to contact anyone outside of walkie-talkie range since early in the uprising when the prison phones had been destroyed and they were determined to bypass Montoya's obvious shine-on of their demand for a conference with the state's top man and the news media. They told the Governor the riot was started "just to get somebody's attention," complained that they were being treated "like a bunch of kids,"[5] and again asked for the opportunity to discuss their grievances with him, Deputy Warden Montoya, Deputy Corrections Secretary Felix Rodriguez, and the media. Governor King promised to set up a table for such a conference in the prison yard an hour later. The rioters in turn assured him no one was going to be hurt and they would give up the hostages by "three or four o'clock" that afternoon.[6] The Governor reiterated that the prison would not be stormed. In spite of the inclusion of Montoya in the conference request, after the conversation with King, one negotiator called the deputy warden and cancelled the invitation. "I talked to Bruce [King] a while ago and he said he was going to come down here and I would appreciate it if you didn't come down here with him."[7] Hearing this, other rioters with radios chimed in with their feelings about Montoya: "You've got fucking uncles, you've got brothers, and you've got cousins all working in here and that is bad."⁸ Through it all, Montoya stayed calm, responding only in the soothing manner he'd learned so recently at "hostage school."

When inmate runners brought out their first list of demands and gave it to Felix Rodriguez at the front gate, negotiations for the day began in earnest. The cement walkway from the prison building to the tower gate became the bargaining lane, where riot negotiators were guaranteed safety to talk with officials through the crosswires of the perimeter fence that separated them. This first list contained six demands:

1. Reduce overcrowding
2. Comply with all court orders
3. No charges to be filed against inmates
4. Due process in classification procedures
5. Ten gas masks
6. Two new walkie-talkies⁹

They were given ten gas masks and promises to consider the rest. The negotiators also requested that a doctor be sent inside the building to care for the ever-mounting number of injured; even Captain Roybal joined in this request, but Montoya insisted the wounded be brought out for treatment. He did allow fire-fighters to go into the yard to put out the fire spreading through the administrative area, but when they approached the windows, they were driven away by rioters stabbing at the hoses with pipes and sharpened broom handles; they even had gasoline thrown on them.

While the institution burned, negotiators were writing up a fuller list of demands, which they handed to Rodriguez that afternoon. This time, officials gathered at the warden's residence to discuss strategy and determine these responses:

1. *Bring federal officials to the penitentiary to assure inmates no retaliation will occur.*

ANSWER: We will ask for the assistance of the FBI.

2. *Reclassify the men held in Cellblock 3.*

ANSWER: Security risks will remain in Cellblock 3.

3. *Leave all inmates in the units they were originally assigned to until the uprising is over.*

ANSWER: We cannot agree to this until the prison's condition is determined.

4. *End overcrowding at the prison.*

ANSWER: About 288 beds will be ready in July and we have asked for an additional 200 from the Legislature.

5. *Improve visiting conditions at the prison.*

ANSWER: This has been in effect for two weeks as worked out with the American Civil Liberties Union Negotiating Committee.

6. *Improve prison food.*

ANSWER: We will hire a nutritionist to oversee the food operation.

7. *Allow the news media into the prison.*

ANSWER: Not until all the hostages are released.

8. *Improve recreational facilities.*

ANSWER: We are now negotiating with the American Civil Liberties Union.

9. *Improve the prison's educational facilities.*

ANSWER: This is being discussed with the Legislature along with raising inmates wages from the present twenty-five cents per hour.

10. *Appoint a different disciplinary committee.*

ANSWER: We will take a long, hard look at that.

11. *End overall harassment.*

ANSWER: We will have additional correctional officers who will be trained. The Corrections Commission is also looking at this problem.[10]

The fact that riot negotiators did not give up the hostages at "three or four o'clock" as they'd promised the Governor speaks for their reaction to these responses. On several points officials missed or skirted the issue. The convicts had not referred to the immediate situation with regard to allowing the media in. They wanted the media to have general access to the penitentiary in the future so that the public was constantly informed about conditions there; as it was, all media representatives were *personae non grata* at Santa Fe. As for improvement in visiting conditions and recreational facilities being negotiated with the American Civil Liberties Union, inmates knew very well from recent experience that such negotiations were time-consuming and when worked out, implementation was resisted by prison authorities. Though the rioters doing the majority of the negotiating knew it was imperative to end the insanity going on around them, they felt they could not give up with so little to show for the hell they'd been through, and the riot raged on.

Meanwhile, at the State Capital in Santa Fe where the Legislature was in the midst of its thirty-day session, Governor Bruce King had asked ten key legislators to interrupt their legislative committee meetings and join him in his office. He needed their guidance on the correction of a decision he'd just made. In the interrogation of escaping inmates, accounts of the killing of a hostage had surfaced. In response to that news, the Governor had given orders to the National Guard and the state police to go in and take over the prison by force. He was waiting verification of the hostage's death to give the final word for the takeover to begin. All the legislators present concurred that he had taken the proper action. If there was killing of hostages, they told him, then it had to be stopped at all costs.

"Well then, y'all go on back to your committee meetings now," he dismissed them in his rancher drawl. "I'll keep you informed as soon as I find out anything. I should know something in thirty-five minutes or so." As the legislators walked out, three of the more progressive stayed behind: state senators Manny Aragon and Tom Rutherford and Lieutenant Governor Roberto Mondragon.

Manny Aragon broke the ice. "Governor, are you going over there to check on what the hell's goin' on, because I'm sure there's a lot of innocent people in there . . . ."

It took only a brief discussion for the Governor to decide to utilize their interest. He appointed the three to go to the penitentiary and act as his eyes and ears, reporting back to him on whether it was necessary to storm the building.

At 3:30 P.M. on Saturday, the three legislators met with police and prison officials at the warden's house to discuss the intelligence collected from the inmates who'd surrendered. By that time, the rumor of a hostage's death had been discounted as false, and the Governor had been so notified. After an hour, they were driving around the perimeter fence of the penitentiary to get a closer look at the damage that had occurred so far. They saw more devastation than they'd expected. From the highway, smoke could be seen coming out of the building for miles, but up close they saw the flames licking up the walls. It looked like a battlefield, wounded inmates being carried hurriedly to the front gate, medics running back and forth with stretchers to bring them to the medical tents stationed beyond the fence, helicopters flying in and out; and framing it all, the forlorn silhouettes of surrendered inmates standing, blankets wrapped around them, like dark ghosts between the perimeter fences. It was five in the evening, the sun had sunk, and the chill of night air was approaching as the three legislators were dropped off at the gatehouse command post. Deputy Warren Montoya and Felix Rodriguez were negotiating face to face with inmates, and the three could hear pieces of the conversation from where they stood inside the building. Soon that little room was so crowded with interrogators, inmates, and other officials, that Senator Aragon decided to brave the night air and walked outside.

Standing against the side of the building, Aragon was just a few feet away from the gateway to the moat where Rodriguez and Montoya stood talking to negotiators on the other side of the fence. At one point, Felix Rodriguez turned toward the Senator and said, "Get me some batteries." Thinking of himself as merely a bystander, Aragon wondered who he was talking to and didn't respond. When Rodriguez again asked for batteries, Aragon realized he was the only person around and hopped to the request, going into the command post and getting a box of flashlight batteries. The guard in the tower opened the gate so Aragon could get the batteries to Rodriguez, who took one

look at them and said, "No, I need *radio* batteries."
Back through the gate Aragon went, coming out this
time with the right thing. When he turned to leave the
moat area, he saw that the gate had been closed and he
couldn't get out, so he stood back against the fence
and watched the negotiations proceeding. Rodriguez
didn't let him remain idle for long. "Get me a
stretcher," he demanded, and again Aragon went
through the gate into the command post, bringing out
two stretchers this time. The gate was opened and he
put them by Rodriguez's side, but once more when he
turned to go, the gate had been locked behind him.
Asking for it to be opened merely so he could get out
didn't cross his mind. The situation was so tense that
the thought of risking security simply for his own
safety didn't occur to him, particularly since he was
able to be of use to the two negotiators. Moreover,
politician that he was, though he felt fear, he was fas-
cinated with the events unfolding in front of him and
not unhappy that he landed smack dab in the middle of
them. As he stood watching the negotiations, it
dawned on him that he knew the two inmates, and one
of them rather well. He'd played Little League
baseball with Lonnie Duran, the jailhouse lawyer
who'd been responsible for writing up and winning a
class action suit against the penitentiary; all three had
grown up in the same neighborhood, the South Valley
of Albuquerque. They exchanged greetings, and soon
Manny Aragon was taking part in the negotiations,
with the blessings of Rodriguez.

The Senator was one of the best aids Rodriguez
could have picked, whether he was conscious of it or
not. Thirty to forty percent of the prison population
came from Aragon's area, and many of his con-

stituents were the fathers and mothers of these inmates. He'd helped many of them get in to see their sons and brothers and husbands in the prison and worked to get children special permission to see their fathers. The convicts knew him to be on their side. At every legislative session he introduced bills that would ease conditions and policies inside the penitentiary. In 1979 he sponsored a bill to study the possibility of conjugal visits or at least furloughs. It didn't pass, nor was his compassionate attitude toward prisoners appreciated by his colleagues, the majority of whom voted the bill down. The preceeding year, he'd introduced legislation calling for a raise in the pay of guards, but that, too, failed to pass, as did a bill to increase the number of parole and probation officers. These hadn't been good issues for him to go on in terms of his political career within the legislative circle, but still, he remained true to his constituency. Now the chickens had come home to roost, and his so-called liberal interest in prisoner rights stood him in good stead. Nevertheless, he pulled no punches in talking to his old pals.

"Lonnie, what're you doing? You guys are crazy. You know you're not going to get away with it. Regardless of how this thing comes down, you know they're not going to negotiate with you on any leniency and stuff like that. I hope you're not involved in it. . . ."

"I'm not. . . ."

"Well, you've got to tell your friends in there that they're gonna get nailed."

"How the hell do I tell them? They'll kill me. It's bad in there; they're killing a lot of people. There's no talkin' to them, they're all drugged up, that's the problem. They're just completely out of it. The only reason they let me out here is because they still remember they respect me, but man, who knows when they'll black out and forget who I am?"

By 7:15 the negotiations had expanded. Rodriguez, Montoya, and Senator Aragon were joined by two newspeople, Santa Fe radio commentator Ernie Mills and Albuquerque television reporter John Andrews. The inmate negotiation team now included two Anglos, Donnie Stout, and Michael Price. The talks became more heated with the addition of the two Anglos, who trusted none of the Man's words and dealt with the crux of both sides' demands: the release of hostages and the meeting with news media. To this latter end, the two reporters had been brought in. Officials were still denying the rioters their desired confab with reporters in front of television cameras but hoped the presence of the newsmen would assuage the negotiators and elicit the release of more hostages.

Ernie Mills, a veteran political reporter in the State Capital, had been at the prison since dawn, the first newsman to arrive. He'd been observing the negotiations all day and had first talked with inmates late in the afternoon. Mills felt a special rapport with the prisoners due to his early background as a street kid in New Jersey; he felt he had some firsthand knowledge of the underdog's mind. He was aware that, with a convict, it was the little gestures that established trust and took the time to establish bonds of confidence by touching the men through the openings of the fence as they spoke and by offering them cigarettes.

Progress was being made for both sides. With the go-ahead from Rodriguez, Ernie Mills promised that a television camera would be brought inside the institution the next day. As a result of this promise, and their trust in the word of both Mills and Rodriguez, the rioters released Lieutenant Anaya, who had been reported in serious condition earlier in the day. At 8:22 P.M., Anaya was brought out of the building on a stretcher. Further negotiations promising a news conference inside the penitentiary that night brought the reluctant release of Officer Juan Bustos, who'd been made to crawl naked in front of the rioters before the control center was broken into at the start of the uprising. Even as the terms for his freedom were being defined, Mills and other negotiators could see the masked inmates guarding the front entrance stab and beat Bustos as others tried to get him through. He was finally brought out into the freezing night air at 11:20, naked and tied to a chair. Seven hostages now remained inside the penitentiary.

Because the mood of the inmates appeared to official negotiators too wild for the press to mix with, the reporters who showed up at the main gate, ready for the promised news conference, were sent back to the highway entrance. Just as negotiations were about to shut down, an NBC cameraman, from Los Angeles, Michael Shugrue, arrived at the gatehouse with camera in hand. He'd missed the first rush and would have been late had the conference actually taken place, for he'd gone to the NBC affiliate in Albuquerque to get a video recorder and camera for the session. Inmates at the gate saw Shugrue and asked if he would be willing to go inside alone and tape a conference with them. Shugrue was willing, providing officials were. "If you want to go in, go ahead,"[11] the deputy warden told him, but not before making a deal for one of the hostages in return for Shugrue's coverage. At seven minutes after midnight, Officer Michael Schmitt was carried out on a stretcher. As the inmates approached the gate, they had a change of mind and, dragging the hostage back toward the building, told Montoya they weren't releasing him until the reporter walked into the prison yard. When Shugrue was in, Schmitt was again dragged to the gate. At first sight of his body, officials thought he was dead. He was laying on his stomach, naked, covered with dried blood. Schmitt was admitted to the hospital alive but in critical condition.

The NBC cameraman spent about forty minutes inside the prison, video taping inmates in the visitors room of the administrative area. Some wore scarves covering their faces, others didn't. They spoke of all their complaints, from poor food to harassment by guards to lack of recreation. While they talked, Shugrue could hear radio transmissions among other inmates warning of violent groups roaming the prison. "Be careful, take somebody that's armed and ready to fight . . . there are two groups in there that are going wild."[12] Killings were going on even as he was taping. True to their word, though, the rioters didn't harm Shugrue. At 7:00 A.M., he was escorted outside and through the yard without incident. "I was never threatened. I never saw a gun or knife, although there were a lot of clubs," he said afterwards. "If I had known then what was going on back there, I never would have gone in."[13]

When Shugrue left, inmate negotiators closed down talks for the night. "Attention all units," they radioed. "We're going to hold off till tomorrow morning. Make sure those guys are fed and nothing happens to them," Chopper One said, referring to the men who'd surrendered. "No hostages will be hurt. We'll start up again at eight in the morning."[14]

Those who'd been negotiating at the gatehouse wearily closed up shop, grateful that they could get out of the bitter cold at last and home to the warmth of a bed. In the moat where the surrendered inmates huddled trying to keep warm under their thin blankets, there was no relief. The stench of corpses that had been brought out of the prison into the yard, together with the smoke from the burning building, kept them remembering what they'd left. As did the screams of that night's victims.

Sunday, February 3, 1980, 6:30 A.M. By the looks of everyone and everything, this riot couldn't go on much longer. Yet, even on this day of Sabbath, the killings continued. Still, the main riot negotiators remained the trusted spokesmen, unharmed and unhindered by the crazier rioters, and those who were tired of the holocaust continued to find their way out through every opening in the building. One group even had the heart to smuggle a young guard hostage out with them, twenty-two-year-old Victor Gallegos, who'd only been on the staff for three weeks. What an initiation he'd had. After being blindfolded and stripped, he'd been placed in a cell with Captain Roybal; Roybal was put on the bed, and Gallegos under it. The cell was locked and they both remained there for several hours, until other rioters smashed the door open and dragged the captain out. "I was praying the whole time," Gallegos later told reporters, "hoping they wouldn't find me."[15] They didn't, but he spent the next hours not knowing what would happen to him. Then the group who got him out of the prison found him, dressed him in an inmate's uniform, gave him an iron pipe so he'd look like the other rioters, and led him from the burning cellblock through smoke so thick "you could only see two or three feet in front of you."[16]

There were so many inmates finding their way out of the institution that one convict was overheard on the radio asking, "What the hell is going on? Where's everybody sneaking out of this place from?" By 8:00 A.M., Sunday, a National Guard commander took a head count and reported that approximately eight hundred convicts were outside the building. Many of those walking or being dragged into the yard were suffering from serious drug overdoses. A few were violently resistant to the medical teams helping them and had to be physically restrained. Helicopters chopped through the air overhead, picking up the wounded and the overdrugged, flying them quickly to hospitals, clogging up emergency rooms with the tatooed bodies of convicts.

I escaped at about seven in the morning by carrying out a wounded inmate. I found his unconscious body on the stairs when I was on my way to take another quick look around. I brought him back into the dormitory and tried to bring him to, but he was overcome by smoke and seemed to be in a bad way. I figured that if I was ever going to get out, this would be the way. Covering my action by announcing that I was going to take the dude down to the information booth and dump him out the front door so he could get some treatment, I put the body on my shoulders and carried it down through the smoke. As I passed the control center, some berserk rioter thought he recognized the guy I was carrying and began swinging a baseball bat at his legs. I didn't stop.

When I got to the information booth, I recognized a few of the white and Chicano clique leaders gathered there.

"Hey, what's goin' on?" one asked.

I played my tough-guy role to the limit. "I got this punk on my shoulder, I think he's hurt. Open the door and I'll bounce him out so's he don't get to stinkin' in here."

"Yeah, that's a good idea, get the motherfucker out of here. Is he dead?"

"Yeah, I think he is," I answered, and without further ado, headed for the door. When I was about three feet out, I yelled back, "I think I'll take him out a little further and dump him there." I walked about fifteen feet into the yard, laid him down on the cement walk, and kept on going. I could hear a couple of Chicanos calling from inside, "Hey, *ese* ["brother"], where're you goin'?" I just kept on truckin', didn't look back or answer, until I heard one of my friends yell out, "Hey, what the fuck are you doin'?"

"I'm goin' out and I ain't comin' back," I said over my shoulder as I neared the gate. "And if you had any sense you'd be out here with me." As I approached the fence where Rodriguez and Montoya stood, I saw others who'd just surrendered laying on the grass face down. I was about to do the same when Rodriguez yelled to me, "Hey, Wally, you and the one next to you, go back and get that guy you brought out and bring him over here." I cursed to myself but got up and did it, wondering all the way if someone would come out and shaft me. They didn't, and we safely carried the unconscious inmate up to the gate, where he was handed through to National Guard medics. The guy helping me laid back down, but Rodriguez told me to

come on out into the gatehouse area. My old case-
worker was there, and he handcuffed me with a piece
of plastic wire and shook me down. Everyone who
came out was getting cuffed, but that didn't make them
feel any looser to me. Marc Orner and Felix Rodriguez
interrogated me. They asked if I knew where the hostages were, if I'd seen them, what it looked like inside,
were there any guns. They told me they'd heard there
were eighty bodies in the gymnasium, but that was
news to me. It turned out that they weren't dead
bodies, just ones unconscious from drug overdoses. I
told them that as far as I knew, no hostages had been
killed. They'd gotten word that Roybal was dead, but
I'd just seen him a few minutes before I came out; I
assured them that there had been no word inside about
the death of a hostage, that the people holding the
guards knew the value of keeping them alive and
feared the consequences of killing them.

When they were finished questioning me, they took
off those painful plastic cuffs and sent me inside the
perimeter moat. A few minutes later, their worries
about Captain Roybal ended. At 8:15, anticipating the
news conference promised the night before, two rioters brought him out to the front gate. While the
helicopter transporting the badly beaten Roybal to St.
Vincent's Hospital whirred overheard, negotiations
for the day began, with Lonnie and Kedrick Duran and
Vincent Candelaria speaking for the inmates and Ernie
Mills, Deputy Warden Robert Montoya, Felix Rodriguez, the brand-new Corrections Secretary Adolph
Saenz and State Senator Manny Aragon on the other
side of the fence.

This session managed to rile the ever-cool deputy
warden, for he was getting a lot of abuse from inmates,

and his tolerance level after thirty hours of tense control was at a minimum. It began with Lonnie Duran telling his friend Senator Aragon that the cause of the riot was Montoya and his practices. This sentiment was borne out by many of the inmates in the yard. On three or four occasions, rioters would come up to the gate and say to one of the officials negotiating, "Okay, you can have your hostages, just give us Montoya." But the encounter that made the deputy warden break from his usual "hostage school" suave came from a rioter who had tears in his eyes when he said, "Montoya, you chickenshit, you're the one who caused all this."

No longer did he suppress his reaction. "You wait till this is over," Montoya answered. "I'll show you what shit can really go down."[17]

Senator Aragon overheard this and turned to Felix Rodriguez. "Hey, Felix, Bobby's losing it; you ought to get him out of here."

Rodriguez agreed, and Montoya left the front gate area. A few minutes later, two more hostages came out. One had been released by riot negotiators, but the other had escaped from the rear of the prison with the help of a group of fleeing inmates. This left only two hostages in the hands of rioters.

At noon, shortly after these hostages were freed, a fight developed in the back of the yard, where rioters who had not surrendered but had left the building had been accumulating. A large group of Chicanos wielding pipes and wooden planks started chasing the blacks, shouting, "Kill the niggers." The blacks ran to the sally port gate with the Chicanos close behind. Police outside the fence told the blacks to drop to the ground. When they did, the Chicanos found themselves staring into the aimed guns of twenty National Guardsmen, with a warning that they had five minutes to retreat or be fired on. To the amazement of the Guardsmen, Superintendent of Correctional Security Manuel Koroneos intervened on the Hispanics' behalf, physically stepping in the line of fire between the guns and the inmates. The deputy sheriff in charge of the law enforcement officers had to tell him to move or suffer the consequences before he'd leave. The Chicanos, bolstered by their homeboy security chief's action, still hadn't given up their position; it took another warning from the deputy sheriff and another look down the twenty gun barrels for them to disperse. The blacks were then taken out of the yard and kept in an isolated section of the perimeter moat. This didn't stop the Chicanos or the whites from coming by and slinging verbal abuse and often dirt and rocks at them. In a bizarre orchestration of movements, just after this melee quieted down, the beheaded body of the only black killed in the riot, Paulina Paul, was brought out on a stretcher and placed against the side of the building with his severed head staring grotesquely between his legs. "If you don't get the media in here soon," the rioters who'd carried him out warned officials, "the next one we shove out will be one of your guards and he'll be just like him."

Within an hour the negotiators had the televised news conference they'd been demanding for the past thirty-four hours. Ernie Mills and a cameraman from the local public television station set up in an office in the gatehouse. Participating were inmate negotiators Lonnie Duran, Vincent Candelaria, and Kedrick Duran, along with four local reporters besides Mills, and intermittently, Felix Rodriguez. This was not the normal television interview, but an informal *"TV verité,"* with the three inmates voicing their concerns in tired, often slurring, voices. Obviously the lack of sleep had gotten to them; in one case, perhaps drugs, too. All three sported mustaches, wool hats pulled over their ears, and prison-issued jackets. Throughout the session there were doors opening, people talking, and the punctuating sound of hiccups. Ernie Mills functioned as moderator, but there wasn't much moderating. The camera was turned on and the inmates took their turns talking through it to the public, who would see the uncut version on that night's news.

Lonnie Duran, the main negotiator, launched the program. "The whole trip was, it wasn't an escape trip, it was just a trip to show the institution that we were not an evil mob. They were treating us like little children when we're grown-up men."

"In other words, we're just tired of all this harassment, harassment, harassment; and it's not that they harass everybody, it's just a select few that they're just getting down on. Like, this is my second time here. When I was here the first time, I was harassed and harassed until I finally made a parole and got out of here. Now that I came back, I tried to do the best I could, but no, they wouldn't let me, they had to knock me off and knock me off for bullshit that I had nothing to do with. I wouldn't even go eat just to keep away from them."

"Another thing that has been brought up," Lonnie Duran took up his friend's thread of thought, "is they're trying to keep people in permanent segregation, as a program, but there's no college program in there, no good time program, there's no program in there but bunk. I can see it if you commit a crime inside the institution, well, that's okay for it, but when you can get picked up for nothing without a report, well, then it's kind of hard for you to understand, it keeps you in limbo there, you know, like, two or three weeks you don't know what's happening then all of a sudden they come and say, well, you're turned loose. But, I don't think that's fair at all. If they got something on you, let's go do it and get it over with, but all this stuff about investigation just doesn't hit the spot."

"What's wrong with this penitentiary, I'll be truthful with you, is there is too many Indians and not enough chiefs. . . ."

"There's too many chiefs and not enough Indians," the third negotiator interjected in a slurring, hardly distinguishable voice.

"Well, all right, too many chiefs and not enough Indians, but I mean each captain has their own set of rules. At one time it was run by one captain and it ran smooth; under Mr. Rodriguez, when he was foreman, this penitentiary ran smooth. It was a great loss to us when we lost Mr. Felix Rodriguez. By all means, I know he won't take a demote in pay, but we need somebody with Mr. Rodriguez's caliber to run this penitentiary."

"I think pretty much that the three people involved in here have the same feelings as most institutions. All of us have been through it. Everybody's been griping about the same things, maybe if we got it cleared up it would be a lot better for all the institutions."

"How much of the penitentiary would you say is on fire?" a reporter asked.

"It's a total disaster, let's put it that way," Lonnie answered. "It's a total disaster because of the water leakage. The main water valve has burned, and there's water in every tier, except on the higher tiers, but there's water everywhere. You've got to walk through water."

"On the way out here right now," the slurring-voiced inmate droned on, "there's a man in between the two grills of the control center; I believe he's dead."

Again Lonnie continued his friend's train of thought. "You can tell by blood all over his face. But I know a personal friend of mine who died of smoke inhalation trying to get back to get another guy out, Frank Sedillo. He tried to go back to get somebody out and he's dead now. They still haven't, as of right now, taken him out. And I'm going to ask Mr. Felix Rodriguez, I'm pretty sure he'll give me permission, to get nine stretchers. We'll have to make a double take on that because there's about eighteen who are dead, and the hostages are doing fairly well. I go every ten minutes, fifteen minutes, to check on them. I don't run nothing in this penitentiary, I'm just doing my time, but yet, because I've got a college education, the guys want me to become the mediator. . . ."

"The reason for the three of us to come in here is because we've been here a while and we've seen the changes that come down. It's not that we're something out of the ordinary, it's just that not too many people like to come and talk to the Man or anything, see? But if somebody don't come and do it, then it's got to be. . . ."

"They're gonna just resort to more killing and I think there's been enough of this," the slurring negotiator interrupted. "Personally, myself, I don't want to see no more killings. I'd like to just get all this taken care of the soonest possible, the easiest way possible, without no more rioting."

This time the main negotiator changed the subject. "I go to mediation meetings once a month, and Mr. Rodriguez proposed this in our mediation hearings, but the Department of Corrections at the time didn't go along with it: Under Mr. Rodriguez's rule they had school release, work release, rehabilitative courses; this is what the penitentiary lacks, rehabilitative courses. Right now they've got a six-month waiting list to see a psychiatrist, and there's guys in there that are walking around like zombies; they've got them up on Thorazine, or whatever it is, walking like zombies that actually don't belong in the penitentiary; they belong in a mental institution. What I'm saying is, it kind of hurts me, because this renovation that's gone on, it's gone to the birds now because of what's happened. There's knee-high foot water all over the place. . . ."

Ernie Mills broke in to tell them what they were filming would be available not just to Channel 5, the public television station, but to all the networks "as long as that's what you guys want."

"As long as it's known that we are not the ringleaders. . . ."

"In fact, the three of us were in Cellblock 3 and we were brought out. Wherever it started, I don't know who or where. . . ."

"You say you were brought out by other inmates?" a reporter asked.

"By other inmates. The three of us were all in Segregation, Cellblock 3. I still have my segregation coveralls on. I was on the north side, bottom tier, and he was on the south side."

"I was in the basement, what used to be Death Row, that's where I was at."

Lonnie explained. "See, a lot of things you can't get around. . . you've got to watch out for your own interest. Even though you try not to get in deep, or at all, you're trying to do what's impossible, its like sometimes you don't want to hook somebody, see, and you turn the other cheek and he still hooks you, see. So what are you gonna do?"

"Most of the guys feel the way you do about Felix?" Mills asked Lonnie.

"Yes. I believe I have Mr. Rodriguez's word and Mr. Montoya's word for no retribution or whatsoever, and I'm gonna take it at that."

But the other two negotiators were intent on clearing themselves. "We were in Cellblock 3 and we were fast asleep when we heard this noise. They opened our doors, they told us: 'You come out and join in or you know what's going to happen.' We're just following our interests, you know. . . ."

"Like, there's no way that we could have kept ourselves in the cell because they had cutting torches, and you'll see once you get inside, a lot of the cell bars are cut."

Ernie Mills got back to the point of the negotiations. "What do you think the chances are that some of the hostages will come out when you go back in there after this?"

"They said they don't want to release the hostages, not unless they get to talk to the news media and Governor King."

"Is there any way possible that we can get a lawyer in here, make this all legalized?" the slurred one had the presence of mind to ask Rodriguez, who'd just come through the door. "That way, if something comes down—I'm not saying that maybe you'll go back on your word, 'cause I doubt it, or Mr Montoya; but it always looks better in black and white where we can say, well, lookit here, this is what they gave us, it's not just hearsay. You know what I mean? If you could arrange something like that. . . ."

"Well, if we do this," Felix responded, "whatever we negotiate at that time, then you guys would release hostages?"

Lonnie answered for the group. "True, I'll do my damndest to have them released."

This wasn't the voice of all three, however. "Once we release all the hostages, then we don't have no play besides your word," one of them complained.

Felix stoically agreed that was the case.

"Plus the fact that we're here," a reporter offered.

"And Felix hasn't gone back on his word with me yet," added Mills.

"Well, were you here the last time, when the men were marched, then stripped, with their hands over their head and everybody just hit them with billy clubs? Well, that's what happened the last time, that's the kind of retaliation that these inmates don't want. If they want to lock us up, lock us up and then later on we'll straighten out our differences."

On hearing that the tape was about to run out, one of the negotiators brought up the injured inside the building. "There's men inside who need medical attention right now. There's about fifteen dead and about six injured that need sutures on their face; they're bashed in pretty bad. I know one who's soaked through two towels already. I told him, 'You need stitches on that, man.' He said, 'I can't go, they'll shoot me.' Right now while we're sittin' here there's probably killing going on. . . ."

"I would like to see if I can get approval to get some guys to get some dead people out of there," Lonnie

Duran asked. "To get the inmates to get the people out of there, and the hurt people."

Rodriguez gave him the go-ahead, saying he could have all the stretchers he needed.

A reporter asked the group at large, "Have you felt that your life has been threatened throughout the last twenty-five to thirty hours?"

"Well, I've really been trying to take care of the hostages," the slurring voice answered. "I was running back and forth to Cellblock 3 trying to get them towels, coffee, whatever they needed."

"The officers that are in our custody right now are most of the old-time guards that we know pretty good and they always treated us right; that's the reason they're getting treated right."[18]

The staccato whirring of a helicopter hovering overhead marked the end of the film. The camera was reloaded and, along with reporters and negotiators, moved to the sidewalk inside the prison yard in anticipation of the release of the hostages and the riot's end. There were still more points the inmates needed settled, however. Joining Candelaria and the two Durans were inmates Michael Colby and Bill Stevens, whose main worry was retribution after the riot.

"One of our demands now is that the five of us that you've talked to are in jeopardy right now, no matter what they say," Colby told reporters. "Once you people leave and they go in there, they're going to beat us and beat us bad."

"It's on the camera and it's in the paper," Mills tried to assure him.

Rodriguez, too, addressed the cameras and reporters. "We will get the hostages out here; I have assured Colby and Stevens, the two Durans, and Candelaria that they will be transferred out of state tomorrow."

"And also that those who stay behind. . ."

"Won't be hurt," the ex-warden completed Colby's thought.

"No segregation?"

"Not at all."

"You can't put people in Cellblock 3 because there's no Cellblock 3 there. . . ."[19]

A few more minutes of haggling and everything was settled. The rioters could have what they'd asked for. Officials would do all in their power to transfer all negotiators to out-of-state prisons as soon as possible; nobody would be strip-searched or beaten after the penitentiary was taken, all in return for the remaining two hostages. The five negotiators were to ask everyone to come out of the prison, move up to the gate, and bring the hostages along with them. Then, one dormitory or cellblock at a time would be told they could return to their unit and pick up their personal belongings. With these points agreed on, Duran and company went back into the building to explain the deal to the approximately 125 inmates still inside. Soon they started coming out with the two hostages in the front lines. But a helicopter swerved in and hovered low over the yard, triggering their inbred distrust of the Man. Thinking they were being set up and were about to get shot down, the convicts started running back into the building, dragging the hostages with them. "You lied to me, you lied to me," some of them shouted. The gate was open, and Senator Aragon ran into the yard, took off his jacket, and flagged the helicopter away; official radios, too, were busily trying to connect with the pilot. Finally the chopper lifted and whirred off, but by that time the inmates were back inside the penitentiary. Colby, Lonnie Duran, and Stevens came out, angry. "What kind of shit is this, you fucker? What are you tryin' to pull?" they asked Rodriguez and Aragon.

"Hey, we don't control those guys," the Senator explained. "Look at this place, it's a goddamned circus. We've got every branch of law enforcement in the state here; they're more disorganized on this side of the fence than you guys in there. Nobody's ready for this thing. The National Guard is marching around to keep warm, and every time they move, you guys get worried it means an attack. Give us a break. You're hearing it from us, you're not going to get hurt, you're not going to get strip-searched, nobody's going to beat you."

It took forty-five minutes to get another agreement, but this time there was an additional proviso. "Before we tell you guys what's going on, we're going to go get our personal belongings first and come out; that way we can see what's going on. Then you'll get your hostages."

The first of the five negotiators out of the building were Lonnie Duran and Vince Candelaria. The two remaining hostages were brought out to sit in front of the prison, blindfolded, their hands tied behind their backs, surrounded by armed, masked rioters. Adolph Saenz, who'd been corrections secretary for just two days, suggested to Rodriguez that it would be a good idea to talk to Duran and Candelaria by themselves, away from the influence of the hardcore attitudes of Colby and Stevens. Rodriguez, who had been worried that Duran and Candelaria were losing their control of the negotiations, took the suggestion and called the

two over to him. "Look, you know what's coming
down. We've got an agreement, there's no problem,
but before Colby and Stevens come out here and start
raising hell again, why don't you guys get the last two
hostages, turn them over to us, and then it's over."
The two thought about it a minute, then walked over,
took the hostages from the surprised inmates, and
brought them to Rodriguez. The gate was opened, the
hostages came through; Rodriguez asked the two
negotiators, "You want to come out now, too? It
would be better for you if you did." And they did. The
armed inmates who had been guarding the two hostages realized they'd been double-crossed and started
yelling at Duran and Candelaria: "What the hell is going on here, you fuckers? You lied to us." Senator
Aragon answered for his friends. "Hey, man, it's over.
All the hostages are here, you can see it's over. You
guys would be smart to put your stuff down, too.
You're better off over here than in there." They resisted for a few seconds, then saw the wisdom in the
suggestion, and came out. As to whether Duran and
Candelaria betrayed the inmates, there was question.
Warden Griffin and Deputy Warden Montoya said
they thought they had, but Rodriguez didn't. "By that
time everybody was fed up with the whole thing. The
smoke was really getting a lot of these people. They
were just as tired of the damned thing as we were."[20]

When Colby and Stevens came out of the building
five minutes later, they felt betrayed. As they walked
up to the front gate, Colby, with a baseball bat in his
hand, was greeted by the hard words of Senator Aragon: "Hey, Colby, it's over. The hostages are all out
now."

Colby dropped his knapsack of personal belongings,

took three steps back, and started yelling for Lonnie and Vince, not believing what he'd heard. When the truth of it sunk in, he screamed furiously at the officials in front of him, *"You lied to us! We're going back in!"*

Rodriguez took control. "Colby, . . . you got a deal, we're going to live up to it, but if you start yelling for those guys to go back inside that penitentiary, these guards are going to blow your heads off. We don't want any more trouble. It's over. Just go sit down over there." It took a few more minutes of yelling back and forth, but finally Colby and Stevens reluctantly put their weapons down and accepted the inevitable. As state police and National Guardsmen rushed through the gates to overtake the prison, the last radio transmission was heard. It was Spanish, between two inmates known only as Danny and Big Al: "The stupid asses gave up the hostages. Now they're going to come in and shoot us. I'm up to my neck in this. If I'm going to die, I'm going to die like a man." Then a few minutes later, the same voice said: "They got us, Big Al. They got us good. They're lined up about thirty yards from us. If you can get word to the people inside, tell them to get out of there." Then Danny was heard talking to other inmates: "When we needed you guys, you turned your back on us. Now you're going to suffer. Tell them guys [presumably the Chicano negotiators] never to call me homeboy again or they're dead."[21] .

What National Guardsmen saw when they went into the penitentiary caused one of them to remark to a reporter afterwards, "I was in 'Nam for two years, and like I've seen some hellacious sights over there, and it's my personal opinion and belief that these inmates

out here made 'Nam look like a playpen."[22] The building was demolished. The mesh-reinforced concrete
walls had been pounded in to make holes so the rioters
could travel through the prison during the last hours of
the riot; fire and water damage had ruined the electronic locking mechanism of the north wing grills and
they were jammed shut. Thick plate-glass shards were
all over the main reception area; the air was filled with
smoke and ashes; floating in the ankle-deep murky water police found many corpses, gruesome sights with
heads so bashed in they were unrecognizable. But in
Cellblock 4, the stench and sight was the worst.
Senator Manny Aragon had followed behind the first
contingent of Guardsmen along with a small group of
civilian observers. When he reached Cellblock 4, he
didn't go in. One look was enough to turn him around.
He didn't see the charred remains of bodies, the blood-
splattered walls, the thick pool of bloody drag marks
leading from the back of one cell to the railing outside;
nor did he see the oddity of Cell 10, with its neatly
made bunk bed, blanket tucked perfectly around the
corners of the mattress, a picture-book reality that had
no place in the carnage surrounding it. Instead, the
Senator made his way down the endlessly long, dark
corridor: dark because fire and water had short-
circuited the electricity. He walked through the smoky
hallway, sloshing through the water, climbing speedily
through the holes in the wall that were the sole access-
way to the front entrance, stopping only when he was
safely through the yard and out the gate.

After thirty-six hours, the bloodiest prison riot in the
nation's history was over. Thirty-three inmates were
dead, all at the hands of their fellow convicts, and
more than a hundred were hospitalized. God knows

how many more were mentally and emotionally Straumatized by the experience. Nowhere in the annals of prison uprisings in this country has there been such an incidence of inmate-to-inmate violence. Even at Attica, where the 1971 riot left forty-three dead, only three inmates were killed by their fellow convicts.

It wasn't over for the relatives of those inmates, though. They'd been standing vigil in the freezing temperatures since dawn Saturday, waiting at the front entrance of the prison near Highway 14 to hear how their loved ones were, if their brother or husband or father was dead or alive. They'd watched the black smoke billow out of the building a quarter of a mile away, their fears mounting as each hour ticked by with no news. They'd taken to mobbing every ambulance and car that came and went through the entrance, hoping to get some shred of information. Two hours before the riot ended, the Governor's press secretary posted an incomplete list of inmates known to be alive. Shouts of joy and wails of grief went up as the list was read. A woman who didn't find her brother's name on the list cried out, "*Ohhh,* my brother's dead."[23] She was comforted by the reassurance of others that it was too soon to tell; all the names had not been given. By, Sunday afternoon, their grief had turned to anger. Homemade signs of protest were made and held aloft along with their shouts: *"No more Atticas!" "Protect the prisoners!"* That night a corrections official read off a list of names over a public address system. He announced that the list was of those alive, but many couldn't hear this, and when the name of their relative was called out, they started weeping and shouting.

This list, too, was incomplete, going only to the letter *G*. One woman moaned, "How long, how long will it be, where is my brother?"[24] They would hold three more days and nights of vigil, huddling together for warmth and courage, accompanying each other to remote places where they could urinate or defecate in some privacy, for there were no toilet facilities nearby, only the wide expanse of desert and the two-lane highway. Not until Monday, when the pleas of priests reached the ears of prison authorities was the Red Cross brought in with portable bathrooms and some food. On Monday and Tuesday nights officials came out and read another incomplete list of those alive, and again many broke down sobbing, either because they didn't understand what the official was saying or because they didn't hear their relative's name and thought him dead. At least two families discovered the deaths of a son and a brother from a newscast before they were notified by prison authorities, and a final accounting of those alive and those dead wasn't completed until March 6. As a clergy member commented, "They just hadn't thought about the families."[25] Such are the desserts of war.

_____ X _____

At night I can still hear the screams, and the smell of burning flesh still lingers in the back of my mind. . . The next time our cries will be heard throughout the heavens above, and society will have to pay the price along with us.

—LETTER FROM INMATES OF THE
PENITENTIARY OF NEW MEXICO[1]

An anthropologist—mind you, an *anthropologist!*—and eleven of his students were called in to search for fragments of human bones in the six inches of ashes and rubble that covered the burned-out gymnasium's floor. The office of the medical investigator had put into operation its "disaster plan," designed to go into effect only when there were "three or more bodies that cannot be visually identified because the remains are skeletonized, badly decomposed, burned, or mutilated."[2] Never before in the five years since its inception had there been a need to put the plan into action. Besides the anthropologist and his eleven students, six dentists, the state's chief medical investigator, and many of his pupils worked around the clock, taking as many as ten hours on each of the thirty-three autopsies they conducted. A refrigerated truck was parked outside the State Laboratory to temporarily store the corpses until the busy pathologists could dissect them. Autopsies usually take no more than two hours, but "because each body was that of a homicide victim with two or three assailants," Medical Investigator Dr. James Weston explained, "I knew that we would need to keep track of lots of evidence. First-degree murder charges will be filed in every one of the cases. All of our findings are going to be presented in court as these cases go to trial."[3] As to the motivation behind the brutal killings, Weston said, "The overriding picture that I got was absolute, unbelievable rage."[4]

In the yard where the surviving inmates lived for three days after the riot, the rage had not subsided. On Monday, February 4, fifteen convicts had to be taken to St. Vincent's Hospital as the result of overnight beatings, stabbings, and one gang rape so severe it left the victim in shock and emotionally scarred for months. The paybacks for non-participation in the uprising had begun; prison sex continued as usual. As well, there was the fear of the men who'd made up the execution squads. Some of those suspected in the killings had been locked up inside the prison in the relatively undamaged Cellhouse 6; others still mingled in the yard. They knew many inmates had been questioned by state police but had no way of divining who had talked about what they'd witnessed. Convicts from Cellblock 4 who'd been willing to give names and details were being kept either in the Annex or other jails for safekeeping, but many more who'd furnished information were still in population.

The conditions they were living under out there did nothing to alleviate the turbulence the prisoners felt. They had no shelter except the thin green army blankets supplied by the National Guard, and the first night there weren't enough of them to go around, another reason for fights and stabbings: "Give me your blanket or I'll pull your throat out." On Monday, when reporters came through to make a tour of the prison, the inmates complained to them that they lacked food and medical attention. "We got the blankets thirty minutes ago to make it look good for the press when they came in," one man shouted. "We've been out here three days with one hot dog." Another said all he'd had to eat or drink was one cup of water since Sunday."[5]

On Tuesday, Deputy Warden Robert Montoya let the leash off his own rage. Forgetting that he was surrounded by more than his protective clique, he let the state police, who were guarding the prison, witness him at his best. Four inmates, who were about to be rehoused in the penitentiary—as units were made accessible, the men were assigned to them—refused to go back, taking up wooden planks to aid their resistance. It wasn't just the memories the building held. They told police that they "feared for their lives if they went into the prison because they had spoken with state police interviewers."[6] Montoya joined with state police to get the planks away from them, and a skirmish developed in which Montoya was hit on the leg with one of the boards. Finally the convicts were subdued and their arms handcuffed behind them. Two state policemen flanked each of the men and began escorting them into the building when the deputy warden stepped in front of two of the inmates, Billy Battenfield and Mark Haddenham. He slapped one of them in the face twice, "screaming at the subject . . . and saying how he would teach him not to hit an officer," State Police Sargeant Billy Holder told Attorney General investigators. Then he ordered the removal of Battenfield's shoes and proceeded to stomp on the handcuffed inmate's stocking-clad feet, saying, according to a prisoner who witnessed it, "Does that hurt? I'm gonna make sure you do the rest of your time in lockup." A former state policeman, Kenneth Thompson, also witnessed Montoya slap and stomp on the two convicts. "Thompson recalled that someone yelled from inside the prison to 'knock it off' because legislators and American Civil Liberties Union lawyers were on tour," the Attorney General's report on the incident said. Thompson also told investigators that "both this incident and another one or two I witnessed involving Bobby Montoya is kind of typical of his attitude toward the prisoners."[7] Montoya denied any wrongdoing, though the Attorney General's report "suggests—but does not conclude—that he tried to cover up his actions and later withheld information from investigators."[8] These findings weren't released until July 31, 1980, but when they were, Montoya's reign inside the Penitentiary of New Mexico ended. Only inside, though. He wasn't fired from the Corrections Department, only placed on leave, with pay, until another position could be found "where the state could continue to utilize his administrative abilities," as the corrections secretary at the time phrased it in a press release.[9]

By Thursday, February 7, 496 inmates were rehoused in the eight dormitories and three cellhouses that were habitable. Another 470 were transferred to federal and state prisons across the nation, from

Leavenworth, Kansas, to Atlanta, Georgia. Those who, like me, had already been granted parole and were doing only waiting time, were released before the end of February.

For the inmates who stayed in the penitentiary, life in those first weeks was abysmal. Those kept in segregation lockup were so outraged by conditions that they set fires and flooded their cells. The men in one of these cellhouses went without water for fifteen hours. Because most of the toilets were smashed during the riot, prisoners had to depend on guards to let them out every time they needed to relieve themselves. But the guards didn't let them out. "To hell with you guys, you wrecked the place," one of the state police officers, supplementing the prison staff, heard a guard tell an inmate.[10] Since nature is irresistible, the inmates had no choice but to piss and shit right there on their cellhouse floors. Only when ex-Warden Felix Rodriguez was informed of this did the situation change. He had to order Superintendent of Correctional Security Manuel Koroneos to provide the residents with access to toilets; thereafter state policemen escorted one at a time to a bathroom whenever necessary.

Of course, on one count, the guard was right; they had wrecked the place and made it the unsanitary, battletorn shell it was. Whether it served them right to suffer or not, they did. Because the kitchen had been demolished, food was prepared at the National Guard Armory eleven miles away in Santa Fe, transported to the institution, and served to the men in their cells, those same cells where the floors served as toilets. Naturally, the meals were never hot, nor were they served at regular times, a major frustration when the monotony of the day is broken only by food. Until

mid-April, that's all there was to do; think and eat.
Due to security paranoias and the fact that the visiting
room had been wrecked, the administration was allowing each inmate to have only one visit weekly, with
one relative for five minutes. Their short dialogue was
conducted at the perimeter fence, the inmate standing
in the yard while his visitor stood ten feet away, a
moat of land and two cross-wire fences between them.
Those locked in Segregation were allowed no visitors
until April. Outdoor exercises were stopped until the
spring, and there were no indoor exercises to work off
aggression, either. The gymnasium had been totally
destroyed. Nor were there any education programs to
occupy their minds. Most of the education department
staff resigned after the riot and the education wing was
badly burned. Some correspondence courses were
reinstated in mid-March, but they came in with a
whimper, with less then fifty inmates participating. All
disciplinary reports, grievances, appeals, and good-
time records had been destroyed. This delayed prisoner classification, which affected participation in the
sparse education programs or living unit status as well
as some parole hearings. Thanks to computers, case-
workers could get parole hearing dates and a few other
documents, and together with their own notes and
memories, new records were compiled on each inmate. Those records were no longer kept inside the
institution but in a trailer outside the main perimeter
fence. There wasn't much mail in or out until mid-
April, when the mailroom became operational. What
there was was often illegally detoured by corrections
officers. Correspondence from attorneys is, by Federal
Court decree, not to be opened by corrections staff
except in the presence of the inmate, and then only to

be searched for contraband. "At least one lawyer had his properly marked letter to an inmate client opened and then returned to him without his client's knowledge. . . . A state police officer observed a corrections guard crumple up and throw away an inmate's outgoing letter."[11] The prison industries program hobbled back to its feet two weeks after the riot, but only eleven inmates were involved in it. Damage to the prison industries building and vandalism helped disable the program. According to the Attorney General's report, some of that vandalism was done by "noninmates [who] stole at least $7500 worth of prison and inmate-owned material from the hoppy shop and prison industries."[12] Guards were the probable culprits. Weapons had been found missing from the penitentiary armory at the base of Tower 1 after the riot; to wit, five revolvers, a carbine, and a 12-guage shotgun. The shotgun was recovered from a corrections officer after an internal investigation, and one revolver was returned by a former officer as the result of that same investigation. Where the other four guns went is a moot question never solved. It wasn't likely inmates had them, for they didn't have access to Tower 1. Someone also stole the master key-cutting machine from the locksmith shop; that was never recovered either.

If guards did make off with this property, they no doubt felt justified, given the low pay and dangerous working conditions of the job. Just after the uprising, a group of officers staged a work strike to protest those conditions and the trauma their thirteen co-workers had gone through while being held hostage. On the day the riot ended, these guards handed their own list of demands to corrections officials. Among those demands were requests for a pay increase to $1,500 per month; additional officers, including a provision that two guards be on duty in each tower for all three shifts; and three weeks of academy training, one week of on-the-job training, and two days of in-service training per month. Though the Legislature put through an emgergency bill to raise their pay to $1,000 a month, guards were leaving the penitentiary at a record number. Fifty-six quit after the riot, and interviews conducted by the Attorney General shows that 80 percent of the guards employed at the prison six months later would resign if offered a better job. They still complained about cliques, lack of supervision, and fears about their own safety. The large turnover caused the newly organized Corrections Master Plan Advisory Committee to accelerate the recruitment of correctional officers with a large-scale media campaign, an activity that wasn't as successful as hoped; it only filled twelve of the thirty-four vacancies. Because of this continued shortage of personnel, the administration was still hard-pressed to release guards for training sessions. An August class had to be cancelled one day because prison officials couldn't spare the men from their duty. Class teachers took the matter into their own hands and stood at the penitentiary gates when the guards ended their shifts, asking them if any were willing to be trained on their own free time. Twenty-five of them volunteered.

The thirteen guards who had been held hostage resigned. Eight of them filed legal suits against the State. In a speech in September 1980, prison psychologist Marc Orner said three of them were "vegetables" and psychotic due to the riot and others were mentally ill; the guards who were raped were "totally destroyed as human beings."[13]

The Corrections Department, too, experienced a turnover in personnel. Corrections Secretary Adolph Saenz, who'd taken the job just two days before the riot, was asked to resign by the Governor in June after being in the position just six months. Some said his ousting was due to the machinations of the corrections clique, but there was equal opinion that he was unqualified for the job and never should have been hired in the first place. There was some merit to this opinion. Saenz had no experience in the field of corrections per se, though he had worked in law enforcement in other countries as an employee of the federal government. He came under fire from prison reform groups after it was learned that from 1965 to 1969, when working as Chief U.S. Officer of Public Safety in Uruguay, he played a role as advisor to Uruguay police, at the time criticized by Amnesty International for torturing political prisoners. In addition, Saenz was censured for creating a new job for his nephew within New Mexico's Department of Corrections, which he supervised. If these things are true, it's a wonder he didn't last; the clique should have welcomed such a sympatico game player with open arms.

Besides Deputy Warden Montoya, two other members of the clique were ousted from the penitentiary, though not from the Corrections Department. Along with Montoya, Superintendent of Correctional Security Manuel Koroneos and the hated "Greeneyes," Lieutenant Benito Gonzales, were transferred to the central office of the department. According to the Attorney General's report, "The new duties of Montoya, Koroneos, and Gonzales are not clear. One member of the Corrections Department remarked, 'No one knows what they're doing here. We don't know if they're being punished or rewarded. All we know is that they're sitting behind desks collecting hazardous duty pay.' "[14]

Other old-timer cliquers remained, like prison psychologist Marc Orner. In spite of the fact that his use of plaster body casts and the deplorable condition of psychological services in the penitentiary came to the public's attention through investigations by the American Civil Liberties Union, no one sought to fire Dr. Orner or to remove him from the institution. The exposé of his operations wasn't the only slur Orner weathered. The Mexican Consul received a letter from him saying that he was seeking to transfer the mentally disturbed Mexican national, Juan Sanchez, to the state hospital "as soon as possible." The strange thing about the letter was that the Consul received it eleven days after Sanchez had been murdered in the riot. The letter itself was dated January 21, 1980, but the envelope was postmarked by the prison meter February 13. There was no chance that it had gotten stuck in the prison mailroom from January 21 through the riot because all mail was destroyed during the uprising. Nor could it have been sitting in Orner's office, for it wouldn't have survived the roaring inferno the psychological unit became during the uprising. Orner offered no explanation until pressed by a newspaper reporter's hounding of the Governor for one. Even then he said nothing himself but filtered his terse response through the prison administrative assistant: He had written the letter, but he didn't recall writing it. Neither he nor the department could explain the twenty-three day gap between when the letter was dated and when it was sent, which led observers to wonder if Orner had been trying to cover his tracks. The Mexican Consul had been inquiring into Sanchez's treatment in the penitentiary in response to his complaints. When it was discovered that no reservation or request for a bed at the state hospital in Las Vegas, New Mexico, had been made for Sanchez, Orner's action began to smell fishy enough for the Attorney General to conduct an investigation. The report made him smell, if not like a rose, little better than the wharf. It found that "there was insufficient evidence to support the charge that the letter was written after the riot and made to appear it had been written before the riot."[15] Still the twenty-three day delay wasn't explained, and still Marc Orner had his job.

There was one fortunate aspect of this riot. It forced the Legislature to allocate more money to corrections than it had in the past ten years. Better late than never. Fortuitously in session during the uprising, the Legislature immediately passed an emergency bill authorizing $87.5 million to be spent on the prison system. Much of this was spent rebuilding the wrecked penitentiary into a medium security prison, and to design a new maximum security facility, for which another $50 million in state bonds was reserved. Funds were also designated for staff salaries and training and to pay the $2.5 million expenses of the riot, which included $1 million-plus for law enforcement services, $1 million-plus for inmate housing in out-of-state facilities, a $190,406.12 hospital bill, and $500,000 for the investigation and prosecution of the perpetrators of the thirty-three murders, thirty rapes and fifteen heinous assaults that occurred during the riot. As many as 125 inmates could be charged with these crimes, according to the district attorney. In addition, New Mexico could have to pay several more million to the relatives of dead convicts who filed lawsuits against the state. The mother of Joe Madrid, the inmate who died helping others escape from the semiprotection unit, was suing for a million dollars, alleging the state failed to protect her son during the riot. Fifteen inmates filed suits against state officials, asking for $1 million each because they "have permanent physical and mental conditions as a result of gross negligence and failure to take measures which were necessary to prevent the riot," as their suit reads. By the time the ninety-day deadline for filing notices of claims expired, there were 412 claims, forerunners to formal suits. Even if the state finds a legal loophole and gets out of paying settlements, it will foot the bill for the court's time, its own lawyers, and witnesses. All this because a decade of governors and legislators didn't listen to the warnings and recommendations of grand juries and so-called bleeding heart liberals when they pointed out the faults in the prison system and the ways to correct them.

And still the misery inside the penitentiary goes on. Residents claim that guards are beating them as payback for the riot. On August 22, 1980, an inmate wrote to the Coalition for Prisoners' Rights in Sante Fe:

> The only way to stop the beatings is to have someone outside able to be contacted at any time and have permission to enter here at any time with a camera. The public defenders took pictures of the guy that got beat. On white guy had a black eye I couldn't believe. It really hurt me to see him in the Hole . . . when I went out to the yard. All this bullshit is going to start another riot. . . . There are still a lot of people working here that should not be. Many people feel that the only way to change a prison system . . . is through violence.

In April, two inmates were stabbed and two beaten in Cellhouse 6, then a maximum security unit, and two food strikes within a week of each other were staged. In the summer, a New Mexico transferee was critically beaten in an Oklahoma prison by another Penitentiary of New Mexico transferee; in August there was a stabbing at Santa Fe. Both victims were reportedly attacked because they'd helped a guard during the riot. In mid-September, I talked with two inmates who were just released from the penitentiary. They told me things were worse when they left than they had been before the riot. The white and Chicano cliques were fighting each other, and the blacks, who were doubly hated for escaping in the midst of the uprising, were kept segregated by themselves. None of the cons were happy with what was going on and there was talk of another riot. As the transferees began to return from out of state and take up residence once again inside the penitentiary, stabbings and disorders increased. On a Saturday night in September, a group of white inmates in Cellblock 6 took over the unit and demanded to speak with Felix Rodriguez. When Rodriguez, who was acting warden, arrived, they returned to their cells after he promised to talk to each of them individually. He kept his word, hearing their fears about being put back into population until 4:00 in the morning, and then again the next day. Two days before, George Saavedra was found stabbed to death in that same cellblock. No murder weapon was found, though everyone was strip-searched and rooftops and grounds were combed. The stabbing death of Saavedra set off racial sparks. Chicanos suspected the Anglos in the cellblock of doing the killing, and inmates of both cliques were concerned that the ethnic balance in the living units might get out of kilter and give one group the upper hand over the other. Some inmates were so worried about the violence going on in the institution that a group of thirty-five wrote "emergency letters" to both the *Albuquerque Journal* and Sante Fe attorney Steven Farber, former head of the public defender's office in Sante Fe, pleading for outside intervention to prevent another riot:

> Everyone knows that it's coming down if no one does something to stop it. . . . The administration that is in control of this prison at the present time is not qualified for the job, and nothing is being done to fix the matter. . . . Right now there is very good reason to believe that there will be another riot. There is tension, anger, resentments. We are constantly being harassed, lied to, the inmates fighting against each other. . . . We plead with you to contact the appropriate people to investigate the further administration of the prison. . . . We the undersigned are sending this letter because we fear that a similar situation such as occurred in February 1980 is building up again here at the prison. There is an extreme amount of tension here. . . . We ask you to please not use our names. You know quite well what can happen to us should our names become public or even if this letter should fall in the hands of the administration.[16]

Attorney Farber contacted the civil rights division of the U.S. Department of Justice in Washington on behalf of the prisoners and, arguing that their civil rights were being violated because they were not being kept safe, asked for immediate federal intervention to allay tensions and for a formal investigation of the way the prison was being run. "If the state can't run the prison, somebody has to," Farber explained his action.[17] The Justice Department was loathe to jump into state business, however, and did not intervene. They did set in motion a mediation team that was supposed to go into the prison and negotiate a peace between the two cliques, but from the look of events they weren't too successful. In October, twenty-one-year-old Apolinar Morago was stabbed to death in the recreation yard outside Cellblock 3. His was not a riot-related killing; he hadn't arrived at the penitentiary until February 11. Still, he was killed with vehemence; multiple stab wounds were all over his body. In this case, too, though a thorough search was conducted, the weapon wasn't found. What was happening to all the shanks? Members of the Criminal Justice Study Committee wondered, too. In an effort to alleviate the problem of weapons being brought into the housing units, they asked penitentiary officials to institute a daily search of inmates working in the prison industries building, where all prison-made knives were created, before they returned to the institution. They suggested that everyone working in prison industries wear distinctive clothing and be strip-searched daily. Having to drop your clothes and stand naked in front of fully clothed guards while they checked out your crevices is a degrading procedure, especially when done by correctional officers who despise you. As Senator Manny Aragon reminded the Committee, the prisoner's personal dignity should be considered. One of the Legislature's more conservative members, who could be counted on to vote against Aragon's many "prison reform" bills, responded, "Whatever inconvenience the prisoners have is a good trade-off for

...ebody's life. The risk to inmates far ex-
...roblem of personal dignity."[18] The Man
...understand what the riot was all about. It's the
lack of personal dignity in prison that makes it dangerous for everyone.

The causes of the February 1980 riot were laid
mainly at the doorstep of management. In a speech
made to the post-legislative conference of the New
Mexico Judiciary on the day his office released a report on the events of the riot, Attorney General Jeff
Bingaman said:

> I think the first part of our report . . . demon-
> strates a pervasive failure of the basics of prison
> management. Before we can take any further
> steps, we need to professionalize the security
> capability of our corrections system. . . . We will
> discover, I think, by applying a strict and more
> demanding standard, that while we have experi-
> ence in our system, as measured in years, what
> we lack is professional corrections expertise.

Whether the man the state hired to take over as
secretary of corrections on November 3, 1980, is an
example of "professional corrections expertise" remains to be seen. The forty-six-year-old cigar-smoking
ex-warden of the Montana State Prison has a history
that makes it an even bet one way or the other. He's
known as a guard's warden in Montana rather than an
inmate's, and in my opinion it's the latter that's
needed in New Mexico. But he's not taking over inside
the prison; he's going to be the guiding light of the
entire corrections network in the state. There isn't a
lot of difference between Roger Crist's regime in Montana and the conditions at the New Mexico Peniten-

tiary over the past ten years. There were middle-management cliques in Montana, too. One guard who resigned in 1979 told the Montana Legislature's Select Committee on Prisons that "a clique of officers like street gangs" controlled the daily administration of the pen by keeping the peace by "pressure and violence."[19] Asked what he was going to do about New Mexico's clique, Crist said he wasn't convinced there was one. He's known Feliz Rodriguez for ten years and is expected to rely heavily on his advice. An old-timer at the Santa Fe institution voiced the opinion that Rodriguez recommended Crist for the job because he thought he could control him. This may not be the way it works out. Crist might not be the perfect reformation man, but he does have a reputation for independent thinking and fairness, so there is some hope. He says of himself, "When it comes to penology, there are two groups of people, those who want to give inmates lollipops and those who want to sharpen their legs and drive them into the ground."[20] He says he falls somewhere in between. He's considered "very fair" by most people who've dealt with him, though. An Indian woman who served on the Montana Crime Control Commission with Crist felt that he always listened to proposals involving minority programs. "Most of the white males on the commission only listened to proposals for guns and flashing lights. Roger would at least evaluate community care programs for Indians and other minorities."[21] On the other hand, a University of Montana sociology professor specializing in criminology says of him,

Roger is a little king at that prison [in Montana]. The Supreme Court ruled that it was a violation to censor inmates' mail. So when inmates receive mail that Crist finds objectionable, he doesn't censor it—he just sends it back . . . A lot of people have come to me and said, "Let's get rid of Roger Crist," but I've never been convinced Roger is the problem. He's done what anybody in that position should do. You put him in the role of a real king, with no controls over him, I don't know what he's going to do. But he just might be able to do the job out there.[22]

His special interest is constructing new, experimentally designed prisons, as he did at the Montana State Prison, a venture that caused critics to accuse him of "empire building." In New Mexico he will have $108 million to create five new institutions by 1990. It is disheartening to know that one of the first appointments he made during his initial month in office was to put ex-Deputy Warden Robert Montoya in charge of overseeing construction of these five new facilities. I do not want to create negativity around Mr. Crist before he begins his work, however. Maybe he will change corrections policy in New Mexico and make the institution more humane as well as more secure. Maybe the riot has shown the legislature once and for all that they can't turn their backs on the prisons any longer. Maybe everyone in corrections will begin to look for programs to teach rather than break a convict.

If I were in charge of designing a new corrections facility, I'd turn the entire system into a "corrections college," a place for the reconditioning and education of everyone who came in, each according to their potential. What was learned in the initial battery of entrance tests would be used to guide the new "student" into one of the many widely diversified courses available. Each living unit would be set up for a particular course. For the person geared to intellectual pursuits, we could have an educational facility. Those more inclined to learning a trade would be placed in a vocational unit, not to make license plates, but to learn a highly marketable trade, such as computer programming. Private enterprise would fund the operation, and the trainees would eventually be doing actual work for the company right there in the unit. At that point, the company would pay him or her a wage, thus keeping the "student" in touch with the everyday realities of the outside world. When you've done ten years earning twenty-five cents an hour, the real world's money scale is mind-boggling. For those more meditatively inclined, there would be a yoga unit, where meditation techniques, Hatha, Yoga, diet, the value of human service work, expanding social awareness, and a sense of responsibility to the community could be developed. In addition, there would be a psychological unit where the student would explore himself as well as study the art of psychology.

Instructors would be the guards, on the premise that it's easier to train a teacher to be a corrections officer than vice versa. This would be the case in all the units; staff would be expert or knowledgeable in the field the unit was dealing with and learn the tactics involved in guarding the security of the institution. In an environment such as this, there wouldn't be danger of an inmate rebellion. The "student" would have an incentive to stay in line. They would be learning something they knew would be of value to them when they got out; they'd look forward to hitting the streets again and trying their new-found talents, so they'd keep their records clean to make sure they go the chances. Training professional instructors to function also as guards would serve to raise the level of correctional personnel within the institution and give the "students" an example of law-abiding citizens that they could not only look up to but desire to emulate.

Even for the 10 percent who were so hardcore they needed to be locked up in a maximum security facility, self-help programs would be provided. Yoga in particular has been effective with prison tough guys and old-timers. "After the first year, we learned that of the thousands of prisoners who wrote to us, most were thirty-five to forty-five years old and had been in prison up to twenty-five years already," a Yoga teacher with the Prison Ashram Project wrote, "or they were people who had been sentenced to two hundred years plus life; people who had less than an eighth-grade education. . . they were desperately grabbing for something to hold on to; something that could help them remain sane and reopen their hearts that had been closed for so many years because of brutality, distrust, and suspicion."[23] The walls of their cells would be painted in calming, unlifting colors, since we do reflect our environment.

"Prison is a holy place," a Hindu Swami said to me once, and I thought to myself, how naïve this guy is. But later I thought about it. Prison *can* be a holy place, a place a human being can be cured of the diseases of their life thus far. Especially now, when the crime rate is as high as is the incidence of low education and poverty in those convicted of crimes; when the money spent annually per prisoner would buy a year at Harvard; especially under these circumstances would I rush to institute my dream "corrections college" and prove what can be done with a progress-inclined outlook rather than one that calls for an eye for an eye. I can only put my dreams to work on paper, but if they really can work, some human being in the field of corrections or with an active interest in the criminal justice problem will flesh them out into brick and mortar. With that hope, I leave you with the wise thoughts of Pope John Paul II:

> The experience of the past and of our own time demonstrates that justice alone is not enough, that it can lead even to the negation of justice and destruction of itself if that deeper power, which is love, is not allowed to shape human life in its various dimensions. In spite of many prejudices, mercy seems particularly necessary for our times.[24]

CHAPTER I

1. From the television documentary, "Death in a South-west Prison," ABC-TV, 1980.

CHAPTER II

1. Tom Wicker, *A Time to Die* (New York: Ballantine Books, 1975).
2. Michael Serrill and Peter Kafel, *Corrections Magazine,* April 1980.
3. "Impact,"*Albuquerque Journal,* June 10, 1980.

CHAPTER III

1. Introduction to George Jackson, *Soledad Brother* (New York: Bantam Books, 1970).
2. Thomas Day, "Behind the Wall, A Most Unusual City, *Albuquerque Journal,* May 20, 1974.

CHAPTER IV

1. From the television documentary "Hard Time," produced by Dave Bell Associates, Burbank, CA 1979.
2. Marc Sani, "Prison Perspective," *Albuquerque Journal,* March 30, 1980.

CHAPTER V

1. From the television documentary, "Death in a South-west Prison," ABC-TV, 1980.
2. Craig Pyes, *Albuquerque Journal,* 1980.
3. Robert Mayer, "The Demon and the Trickster at Play," *Rocky Mountain Magazine,* June 1980.

CHAPTER VI

1. Jessica Mitford, *Kind and Unusual Punishment* (New York: Random House, 1971).

2. From the television documentary, "Death in a Southwest Prison," ABC–TV, 1980.

2a. *Albuquerque Journal*, September 2, 1975.

3. Thomas Day, "Behind the Wall, a Most Unusual City," *Albuquerque Journal*, May 20, 1979.

4. Ibid.

5. *Albuquerque Journal*, September 2, 1975.

6. *Albuquerque Journal*, September 21, 1975.

7. Ibid.

7a. Report of the Attorney General on the Feb. 2 & 3, 1980 Riot at the Penitentiary of New Mexico ("Report of Attorney General"), September 1980.

8. "Death in a Southwest Prison," 1980.

9. Ibid.

10. Report of the Attorney General on the Feb. 2 & 3, 1980 Riot, September 1980.

11. Report of the Attorney General on the February 2 & 3, 1980 Riot—9/80 Jeff Bingaman, Attorney General, State of New Mexico.

12. Ibid.

13. Ibid.

14. Report of the Attorney General on the Feb. 2 & 3, 1980 Riot, 9/80.

15. Thomas Day, "Behind the Wall, a Most Unusual City," *Albuquerque Journal*, May 20, 1979.

16. Ibid.

17. Ibid.

18. Report of the Attorney General on the Feb. 2 & 3, 1980 Riot, 6/80 & 9/80.

19. Ibid.

20. Report of the Attorney General on the Feb. 2 & 3, 1980 Riot, 9/80.

20a. Report of the Attorney General on the Feb. 2 & 3, 1980 Riot, September 1980.

21. Craig Pyes, *Albuquerque Journal,* September 23, 1980.
22. Ibid.
23. Ibid.
24. Ibid.
25. Ibid.
26. Ibid.
27. Ibid.
28. Craig Pyes, *Albuquerque Journal,* September 23, 1980.
29. Ibid.
30. Ibid.
31. Ibid.

CHAPTER VII

1. From television documentary, "Death in a Southwest Prison," ABC–TV, 1980.
2. M. Serrill and P. Katel, *Corrections Magazine,* April 1980.
3. Report of the Attorney General on the Feb. 2 & 3, 1980 Riot, 6/80.
4. Ibid.
5. Robert Mayer, "The Demon and the Trickster at Play in the Bottomless Soul of Man," *Rocky Mountain Magazine,* May/June 1980.
6. Ibid.
7. Ibid.

CHAPTER VIII

1. Jessica Mitford, *Kink and Unusual Punishment* (New York: Random House, 1971).
2. Bruce Campbell, "Prison Perspective," *Albuquerque Journal,* March 30, 1980.
3. "Death in a Southwest Prison," ABC Documentary, 1980.
4. Campbell, "Prison Perspective."
5. Ibid.
6. Ibid.
7. Ibid.

8. Ibid.
9. Report of the Attorney General on the Feb. 2 & 3, 1980 Riot at the Penitentiary of New Mexico, Part II, September 1980.
10. Tom Wicker, *A Time to Die,* (New York: Ballantine Books, 1975).
11. Mitford, *Kind and Unusual Punishment,* p. 00.
12. Ibid., p. 00.
13. Wicker, *A Time to Die.*
14. Ibid — (found in); quote from N.Y. State Dept. of Corrections "Sing Sing Prison: It's History, Purpose, Makeup & Program (1968).
15. Mitford, *Kind and Unusual Punishment.*
16. Ibid.
17. Ibid.
18. Ibid.
19. Ibid.
20. Ibid.
21. Ibid.—"Our Law-abiding Lawbreakers," J. Wallerstein & C. J. Wyle, *Probation,* 1947, "A Report on Crime & Punishment in America," New York: Hill & Wang 1971.
22. Theodore Sabin, *The Myth of the Criminal Type* (Connecticut: Wesleyan University Press, 1969).
23. *The Challenge of Crime in a Free Society,* Report to the President's Commission of Law Enforcement and Administration of Justice, Washington, D.C., U.S. Government Printing Office, 1967.
24. Tom Wicker, *A Time to Die.*

CHAPTER IX

1. Robert Mayer, "The Demon and the Trickster At Play in the Bottomless Soul of Man," *Rocky Mountain Magazine,* May/June 1980.
2. Ibid.
3. Report of the Attorney General on the Feb. 2 & 3, 1980 Riot at the Penitentiary of New Mexico—Part I, June 1980.

4. Ibid.
5. Ibid.
6. Ibid.
7. Ibid.
8. Ibid.
9. Ibid.
10. Ibid.
11. Ibid.
12. Ibid.
13. Ibid.
14. Ibid.
15. *Los Angeles Times,* February 4, 1980.
16. Ibid.
17. Interview with Senator Aragon.
18. Videotape—KNME Public Television, Albuquerque, New Mexico, 1980.
19. Ibid.
20. Peter Katel, "Riot," *Corrections Magazine,* April 1980.
21. Ibid.
22. From the television documentary, "Death in a Southwest Prison," ABC–TV 1980.
23. Associated Press, Feb. 4, 1980.
24. Ibid.
25. Report of the Attorney General on the Feb. 2 & 3, 1980 Riot at the Penitentiary of New Mexico, Part I, June 1980.

CHAPTER X

1. *Albuquerque Journal,* September 24, 1980.
2. Lynn Buckingham Villella, "After the Penitentiary Riot," *University of New Mexico Alumnus.*
3. Ibid.
4. From the television documentary, "Death in a Southwest Prison," ABC–TV, 1980.
5. *Los Angeles Times,* February 4, 1980.
6. *Albuquerque Journal,* July 31, 1980.
7. Ibid.

8. Ibid.

9. Ibid.

10. Report of the Attorney General on the Feb. 2 & 3, 1980 Riot at the Penitentiary of New Mexico, Part I, June 1980.

11. Ibid.

12. Ibid.

13. *San Francisco Chronicle,* September 22, 1980.

14. Report of the Attorney General on the Feb. 2 & 3, 1980 Riot at the Penitentiary of New Mexico, Part II, September 1980.

15. *Albuquerque Journal,* September 1980.

16. *Albuquerque Journal,* September 24, 1980.

17. Ibid.

18. *Albuquerque Journal,* October 1980.

19. *Albuquerque Journal,* November 1980.

20. Ibid.

21. Ibid.

22. Ibid.

23. Interview with Bo Lozoff, "Getting the Word In," *Sufi Times*.

24. Encyclical, December 2, 1980.